After it H.

Book 1: Survival

Devon C Ford

PRESS

Copyright © Devon C Ford 2016

All rights reserved. No part of this publication may be reproduced, stored in or introduced into a retrieval system or transmitted in any form or by any means, electronic, mechanical, photocopying, recording or otherwise without prior written permission from the publisher.

This novel is entirely a work of fiction. Names, characters, places and incidents are either the product of the author's imagination or are used fictitiously, and any resemblance to any person or persons, living or dead, is entirely coincidental. No affiliation is implied or intended to any organisation or recognisable body mentioned within.

Originally self-published by Devon C Ford in 2016
Published by Vulpine Press in the United Kingdom in 2017

ISBN: 978-1-83919-222-7

www.vulpine-press.com

Dedicated to WH: the first person to read this story, if only to be polite.

PROLOGUE

He stood there, breathing heavily. Nervous tension cramped his muscles as he steadied himself.

Under normal circumstances, breaking into a police station would attract at least some attention. He would've been happy in a way if it had; he hadn't seen a living person for hours now.

Smashing the glass doors had made a sound like a shotgun blast, but nobody came to investigate. That was OK. He was there to steal things he needed and didn't really want any complications just yet.

He made his way through the eerily deserted station, through the locker room and upstairs, checking offices and cupboards as he went.

He could already smell it: not decomposing body, just death. It had its own smell, which you either did or didn't get used to. He hadn't yet, after years of the familiar but unpleasant odour, and supposed that he would probably have to from now on. He kept his emotions buried as deep as he could, ignoring all the grief, confusion, and panic.

The drive there was littered with other bodies. Some in cars, some slumped in the road where they fell, but the world was deserted on the whole.

His journey had led him to the police station, where it dawned on him that he had better get organised, quickly, before other people did. The simple fact remained that it was easier to take a gun off a dead person than a living one who could still use it.

He eventually found what he was looking for: A man seemingly asleep on the desk, still sitting on his chair with both arms hanging down by his sides.

A tentative kick to the chair got no response, so he began the task of trying to wrestle with the stiffening body, grown heavy through a combination of weightlifting and dead weight, to remove its belt and ultimately the Glock strapped to its right thigh. Trying not to look at its face was the hardest part.

Eventually he stood there with the gun and holster. He helped himself to the two spare magazines to complete the set.

He took the keys for a BMW from the oversized carabiner on the body's vest and made his way back outside via the locker room. He found some bags containing chemical suits and gas masks, and he picked them up, morbidly thinking ahead.

Using the key, he played car park fishing and the hazard lights of a grey X5 flashed on. Nice for now, but probably not hard-wearing enough in the long term. After another grim corpse dance, he'd retrieved another Glock from the passenger who was still strapped in. A decent burial would've been kind, but time wasn't a luxury he had, so the passenger went out in the car park to be laid in his final resting place on the tarmac.

He shuddered as he realised he recognised the person he had just dumped on the floor to rot. He couldn't remember his name, which made him feel a little shallow. *No time for sentiment*, he thought, *keep it together.*

As luck would have it, the passenger was left-handed. He worried for a moment that having a gun strapped to each leg looked ridiculous, but then he remembered that it was unlikely for there to be anyone around to judge him. Using all the extra keys on the bunch, he finally opened up the locked cabinets in the boot, hoping to find an Aladdin's cave of goodies. Nothing. No big guns.

Shit.

Guessing that all the bigger stuff would be locked away in an armoury he couldn't access, he forgot the thought for now. There was more to life than guns.

Quick inventory: X5 with a full tank, two Glocks with six magazines between them, his own small bag of supplies, and some gas masks for the next building full of dead people. He was also running low on cigarettes. The really good stuff in the boot was the magic door-opening kit: pry bars, hydraulic openers, and the ever-reliable ram.

He threw his own small bag in the back and opened the windows to try and purge the smell. A forlorn look at the diesel pump sitting proudly in the car park made him wonder; he didn't have the knowledge or the tools to siphon it out, nor did he have anything to carry any spare fuel in.

Alone, dazed, and scared, he headed out without really knowing where he was going. He drove aimlessly for a while, ideas struggling to take form in his post-traumatic head.

He stopped on a large, abandoned garage forecourt and tried the pumps. No power. He wandered inside after forcing open the sliding doors and picked up a basket. Strolling from aisle to aisle, he hummed to himself as if he were just grabbing some things in no great rush.

Exactly what he was doing two days ago, in fact, before he got a call from her to say she and the kids were unwell.

The humming turned into a croak, which became a sob. It was all he could do not to lose it right there and then. He screwed his eyes tight shut and forced himself to breathe, trying to forget the last memory of his family.

"There's nothing you can do about it," he said to himself softly, over and over.

It didn't work, and he crumpled to the floor, finally letting the tears and the anger and the fear wash over him.

NEIL

Neil was a broken man. Destroyed. He had cared for his wife and boys all night as they coughed in agony. At first he was worried that all three had displayed the same symptoms, but when they got worse quickly, his concerns became panic.

He was sure they had been poisoned. He tried to think what he had consumed that was different to them, but couldn't think as he was running between them as the horrible, racking, deep coughing fits hit them again in turn.

He called 999 and got an engaged tone. He tried again. On the tenth or eleventh time he tried for an ambulance, he received a dead tone in answer.

He lost control then; he was exhausted and blinded by fear. He ran to his neighbour to ask for help and hammered on his door fit to wake the dead. He got no response, so he ran to look through the only window where he could see light. He saw his neighbour on the floor, clutching his stomach and coughing uncontrollably.

Neil went back to his family. All three were in the lounge where he could look after them all in one place. They were grey-skinned, blue-lipped, and incoherent with pain and exhaustion.

He couldn't understand it; they had all been fine this morning. His thoughts of poisoning had been diluted by seeing his neighbour with the same illness.

Something in the water? No, he had drunk the tap water too that day and he was fine. It couldn't be poison; it had to be something else. Just as he was thinking in between soothing one of them, the lights went out.

Plunged into darkness, Neil cried as he held his family.

One by one, they stopped coughing.

Neil sat there for hours, long after the pins and needles took hold and numbed his legs. He was still sitting there, clutching them, as the sun rose and bathed his family in warm light. They were gone, and he was alone.

Good sense tried to make a reappearance – Neil tried the phones again and checked the fuse box. No phones, no power. He looked through neighbours' windows and found the same tragic story in all of them. He was in a ghost town.

He stood in the middle of the road, which normally would be queued with traffic by now. He turned a circle and bawled "Any-body!" at the top of his lungs, leaving him short of breath.

He was alone.

He returned home in a trance and started to dig three holes of different sizes in his back garden. He was proud of his garden, having spent a couple of years working on it. They liked to sit outside and watch the boys play – or more usually fight – on the grass while they sipped their drinks and relaxed.

Now his garden was three knee-deep rectangular holes. He carried out his wife and his two sons one by one and laid them gently to their permanent rest. He cried aloud again as he filled the earth back in over the holes, patting it down gently, as he didn't want to hurt any of them.

He prised up the decorative paving slabs from the patio he had so painstakingly laid, and paid the same attention to detail as he covered his family as best as he could.

He sat there for hours, watching their graves. He ignored the rumblings in his stomach and the dry burn of dehydration in his throat.

Eventually he stood and marched inside the house with purpose. He went to the bathroom and used cold water and soap to scrub himself clean. The tap spluttered and stopped, making a strange sinking noise reverberate through the house.

No water and no power. He put on some clean clothes and packed a small bag with whatever he could grab, now eager to leave the house and not see the neat graves in his own little corner of happiness.

He got into their car and drove away for the last time.

His wife always scolded him for being inappropriate in bad situations. Neil's way to cope with emotions was to make light of them – not that he made jokes in bad taste to people, more that he acted a bit of a clown to hide how he truly felt.

He looked through the windows of the sixties semi-detached where his parents lived. He couldn't face checking anyone else he knew, nor could he spend his life digging graves for the hundred thousand people within walking distance from where he was. He got back in his car and drove away, trying to leave his guilt there too.

He'd gone a mile or so, stopped his car on a new garage front next to a new BMW X5, and went to get something to eat in response to his growling stomach.

He realised he wasn't the only person alive after all, almost running into the shop with tears of happiness and relief stinging his eyes.

FIRST IMPRESSIONS

He had no idea how long he'd been like that.

Long after, the tears had stopped. He just sat there, catatonic, waiting for an outside stimulus to bring him back into the nightmare of being awake.

"Um, you alright, mate?" called Neil from the doorway.

The man leapt up from the floor, screaming in terror and rage at the surprise. This caused the other man to scream louder and higher and dance on the spot involuntarily until his eyes focused on the gun levelled at him from ten feet away. He became very quiet and still, raising his hands slowly.

"What do you want?" barked the man with the gun.

The newcomer just stammered until he visibly took control of himself. "My name's Neil. I'm on my own. I haven't seen anyone else since yesterday," he blurted out. Then he said slowly, in a very measured voice, "Everyone I know is dead; I don't know what to do, and I was hoping you did." His lower lip trembled with the effort of not crying again.

On hearing this, the man slowly lowered the gun he was pointing at Neil.

What the hell am I doing, he thought. The first living person he'd seen since...since this all started, and he was caught in the middle of a full-blown psychotic episode and responded by pointing a gun in the guy's face.

Nothing like a first impression.

He took a breath and holstered the gun. Neil looked to be in his early forties, short and a bit chunky with very little hair left. He seemed to compensate for this with a blond goatee beard and had the overall look of a nice bloke who was probably quick to smile and laugh.

In comparison to how he looked, Neil was probably the more stable of them. He thought about what Neil was seeing: six-foot-tall white guy; short, greying hair; fit-looking; red-faced; puffy-eyed; and wearing a gun on each leg like he'd played far too many computer games.

He suddenly felt very foolish, almost embarrassed.

"I'm sorry, Neil, you caught me at a bad time," he said in his most businesslike tone. "I was just doing a spot of shopping if you care to walk with me?" He winced, thinking that he'd made himself look a little more like the Mad Hatter than he already did. Maybe just go the whole hog and suggest a tea party?

Neil surprised him then, and in a passable BBC voice, he replied, "Splendid idea, chap, don't mind if I do! I hear this place has become very affordable recently, eh?" he said as he jauntily swung a basket into his elbow.

The man was already laughing before the routine had finished, which seemed to signify that their initial interaction had been mutually ignored. Neil looked at him; behind the teary eyes and laughable holsters, he saw a professionalism hidden behind the failed first impression.

They grabbed drinks and food, avoiding the sandwiches that although still in date looked a little on the salmonella side. The man helped himself to a large amount of cigarettes, threw in all the medication on the small shelf, and then picked up a bottle of Scotch, silently raising it to Neil for approval.

"Good God man, no! From now on, we shall only drink the expensive stuff; none of that rubbish," he replied, still in his best "Rule Britannia" voice. The man nodded assent with a smile and selected the three bottles of single malt whisky instead.

They returned outside and the man saw a rather tired-looking people carrier parked near the X5. He could see kids' seats in the back, and the thought was almost too much.

"Neil," he said, turning away from the cars to face him. "What say you and I travel together, Old Boy?" the accent wasn't as good as Neil's, but the thought was there.

"Capital idea, capital!" he replied in his best approximation of a stereotypical Wing Commander. "Just give me a minute to grab my stuff," he said, dropping the accent.

The man had always been a cynical type: not that great at sharing and not known for his generosity. He had become a bit of a recluse over the last year as it was, and not having been a true people person before, that didn't exactly help his social awkwardness.

The whole world as he knew it had changed, so why shouldn't he at least try?

"Hey, Neil, know how to use one of these?" he called, pointing to the Glock on his left leg.

"Haven't used one since I got out years ago, but I'm sure the fundamentals are the same," he replied.

LAND ROVERS

They woke the next morning with a little more purpose. They packed the car with as much as they could, including more tins and bottled water from a nearby shop, and set out with their plan of building a survivors' society. They decided that the X5 had to go; it was a big vehicle but the boot was modified with stuff for the guns and didn't have enough space.

A set of decent walkie-talkies was found, along with a stack of batteries. Dan tried the police radio in the car, but without power to the systems, the digital network was down.

First stop, proper survival vehicles. They discussed this and without much argument settled on Land Rovers. Ten miles away was a dealership, and after having to reverse the X5 through the big glass doors, they set about car shopping.

Neil had his heart set on a new Range Rover, but Dan argued that they needed to be less bling about their choices and more utilitarian.

He settled on a black one-ten Defender with a roof rack and Neil eventually followed suit and chose a similar grey one. Dan's had a winch on the front, which he thought would come in handy at some point. It took a while to find the keys and tools to remove the wheels from other Defenders and strap them down on the racks so both had another five spare wheels.

They found a few jerrycans in the garage, and Dan helped himself to the speed jack they'd used to get the other wheels off. After he'd almost choked himself on diesel by trying to suck it through the piece of hose pipe, Neil showed him a better way by putting the whole pipe into the tank and putting his thumb over the end before drawing it out quickly. They repeated this until both trucks were full and they carried sixty litres of extra fuel taken from the rest of the stock vehicles.

They'd gathered maps from the camping shop, but both Neil and Dan knew the area anyway. They decided to set up their temporary camp on the car park of a large nearby Morrisons. As they jumped in and started their new motors, Neil called out a warning over the radio.

"I saw someone!" he said excitedly.

Dan looked over to him and saw him pointing straight in front towards some bushes. He drove to the left and into the car park behind the bushes, just in time to see a flash of movement disappearing again behind an industrial unit.

He got out and shouted to whoever it was, "Come back! We won't hurt you. It's OK. PLEASE…"

Nothing.

From what he could see, he had no idea if it was male or female, young or old.

They decided to leave a message anyway, and using spray paint, they daubed instructions to come to the supermarket, giving directions and leaving the keys to the X5 there with a promise to help.

As they drove, Neil called Dan on the radio again from his position behind as they dodged the abandoned cars.

"Mate, there's a caravan place down here on the left, shall we check it out?"

"Sounds like a plan," Dan replied.

Neil had great fun; he moved a few of the smaller caravans around and took the wheel clamps off two big caravans. He hitched them up to the Defenders, clearly having done this before, and gave Dan a quick lesson in towing. It would've been a valuable lesson; however, Neil delivered it in the style of the quintessential travelling gentleman and Dan couldn't really follow much of it.

The word *Dags* appeared once or twice, and there was a mention of what to say if "da po-liss" stopped them, but Dan was laughing too much to take careful note by the end.

They noted the site for a return trip to get more caravans and gas bottles, wishful thinking for finding more people, they supposed. They towed both caravans to the supermarket and parked them up away from the main entrance, which was blocked with abandoned cars. Clearly someone had tried to break in – unsuccessfully, by the look of things.

They set about moving the abandoned cars clear, giving themselves space to set up the caravans. The beauty of driving a Defender was made clear: it was the big bully of car pushing.

Neil was obviously experienced at setting up the fold-out legs. Dan thought that caravan holidays probably meant family, so he kept very quiet.

"I'll go and finish the botch job on those doors," he called to Neil, who just waved irritably, as he was busy winding down the weird leg things.

Give me a tent any day, thought Dan.

He had to use the hydraulic door spreader to get the doors open enough to prise the lock housings out, and was sweating and out of breath by the time he'd finished. He could smell the fruits and vegetables starting to go off already. A quick walk around the shop showed that there was enough food and water to last for months living in their caravans, and now he just wanted to find as many people as he could to join them.

Maybe saving more people would wipe out the guilt of leaving her in bed where she died.

When he got back outside, Neil was finishing connecting the gas bottle to the last caravan and graced him with a loud, cockney "Ta-da!"

Dan in turn produced some tins of stewed steak and potatoes and a box of eggs – mountaineering spew it was again, then.

As they sat in folding chairs by their caravans eating dinner, they discussed the next day's plans.

"We need a lorry. Load it up with all the good stuff from here," said Neil.

Dan agreed that it was a good idea; they needed to find proper supply and scavenging vehicles if the thought forming in his head was to work. But they'd also need a lot more people with them to drive and load those trucks.

"I think we should stay here for a while. The weather will be OK for a few months, and we've got plenty of food and shelter. What we need to do is get out there and get more vehicles and caravans back here, and more people to fill them." Dan paused, unsure if he should voice his ideas just yet. "There have to be more people alive; we saw one at the Land Rover garage, remember?" he reasoned.

"OK, mate, chill out, yeah?" shot back Neil, this time in a convincing Cape Town accent. "Tomorrow. Tonight, we rest and continue our prescribed course of Glenfiddich. Chin Chin!" he said, raising an actual glass this time.

LEAH

She felt cold. She'd decided to sleep in the back of the car the men left. She'd heard them smashing the doors with it and watched them for ages, wanting to go and speak to them. She wanted to burst out in tears and ask for help and tell them she was scared and that her mum and her little brother hadn't woken up.

She wasn't that naïve, really; she knew they were dead.

     ~

The night before, she had listened to her mum coughing all night until she didn't cough any more. Her brother hadn't made a noise for hours, and she knew in her heart that they were gone; she just wasn't brave enough to go and check. Everyone had got poorly, and then they just died.

She lay there all night in the silent pitch-black, the streetlight outside her window having shut off during the night. She'd been inside the house for two days now because everyone was sick. Before her mobile phone lost Wi-Fi and then normal signal, none of her friends would answer her texts or calls.

She waited in bed until eight thirty, as she always did, so as not to get in trouble for waking people up. She wasn't like some other twelve-year-olds; she wasn't feeling the need to sleep all morning like a teenager yet.

She loved her makeup, YouTube, and she lived never more than two feet away from her iPhone. Just like the family members in the house, everything she loved just no longer existed. She was scared, hungry, traumatised and completely alone.

She couldn't force herself to check the other two bedrooms; to see what she knew was in there would just make it real.

Leah tried to be logical. She got a bottle of water from the fridge, which wasn't that cold anymore, and helped herself to the secret stash of chocolate for breakfast. She couldn't quite bring herself to reason that the previous owner had no further need of it.

She sat down and tried the TV. Dead. The laptop. Dead. The Kindle. Dead. Like a typical twelve-year-old, she was already bored. She tried her phone. It had no signal or data, but she played games for a while.

She decided that she couldn't sit there forever with nothing to do, so she got dressed, packed her handbag and another bag with some essentials (make-up, hairbrush, mirror, phone charger), and went downstairs.

She left the house, not bothering with a coat, as it was warm and dry, shut the door behind her, and probably blocked out the fact that she'd never return there again.

She walked into town, bag in the crook of her elbow, iPhone in hand playing some Taylor Swift, with a small sense of normality. She ignored the dead silence that surrounded her and the sight of abandoned cars. The inactivity of the world seemed alien and frightening.

That's when she heard the glass breaking. She killed Taylor quickly and crept up to the bushes where there was a car garage. She saw two men, one tall and dark, the other shorter and fatter with no hair. They seemed to be friends, and they didn't look like paedophiles, but as she was told in school all the time, you don't know what a paedophile looks like and you should never go to strangers without a parent. Well, that clearly wasn't going to happen, and she didn't trust the look of the men enough, so she just watched.

They were in there for ages, and she could hear them arguing about the cars. One said, "Look at this one, though, it's gorgeous." He said *gorgeous* in a funny voice, which made Leah smile.

The taller one, who looked moody and not funny at all, said the other man wanted to be a drug dealer and started taking wheels off the cars. Leah knew drug dealers were bad people, so she thought she'd done the right thing by staying put. The moody one had something on his leg which Leah thought looked a bit like a gun. She knew that guns were illegal, and that worried her.

She watched the moody-looking one nearly throw up when he tried to drink the petrol out of one of the cars, but the funny one showed him what he was doing wrong.

Leah decided that she would just walk past and speak to them, make out as if she was going somewhere. She doubted they were the kind of bad people she was always told to avoid, but you never knew. She probably realised deep down that she had to find some help.

She had nobody left to look after her.

She'd been daydreaming like that for a while when she looked up and saw the funny man looking right at her. The moody man drove his big car fast to where she was hiding, so she ran. She didn't know how far she had gone, but she was gasping for breath and crying uncontrollably by the time she stopped. She thought the moody man shouted at her when she ran away, and decided it was probably a good idea she didn't go near them.

A while later, she walked back to where the garage was and saw that the men were gone. After a time spent watching from the bushes again, she went to see what they'd done and read the note they had painted on the floor: "Survivors at Morrisons – come and join us. We can provide food and shelter. We've left the keys to the BMW – food and water inside."

She assumed that the BMW was the big car they had used to break the doors, but she didn't understand why they took other cars. There were numbers after a capital *A* painted there too, and Leah thought that might be a road or something. She did know a big Morrisons in the next town because her mum took them there when they didn't go to Aldi, but she didn't know how to get there.

She looked around the garage for a bit. Nothing worked, just like at home, but she did find loads of biscuits in a cupboard under a coffee machine that looked like a spaceship. She ate a whole packet and drank one of the bottles of water left in the car.

Now she faced a difficult decision. She thought that the men she saw had scared her, but now that they had left the note, they seemed to want to help. They probably knew what was going on and could help her get to her grandparents' house or something. She decided that she probably had to find other people, and these men had left her water and some other snacks, so they probably weren't going to hurt her.

She made up her mind that she should definitely go and see them at the shops. The only problem being that she didn't know how to get there. The car they left had a big fancy screen, and she thought that might be a satnav. If she could get it working, she could type in *Morrisons* and the road number and it would show her the way.

She went to put the key in the ignition like she'd seen other people do all the time. The only problem was that there wasn't a keyhole, and the car key didn't have a metal bit sticking out. She eventually figured out that the key was like a bank card that you fitted in the slot on the dashboard. She put it in and the blowers started up, startling her.

There was a button that said "START STOP engine," which seemed like a good way to go.

She pressed it and was rewarded with the noise of a six-cylinder diesel firing up straight away. She didn't know this, obviously, but she jumped out of her skin because it sounded like a lorry was in the building with her.

Steadying her nerves, she looked at the gear stick. Grandad's car had numbers on it and she knew you had to put it in 1 and then take off the handbrake. Then you had to do the pedals: change gear, stop, and go. Easy.

This one had letters and symbols and there wasn't a handbrake and only two pedals. She messed around with the controls for a while until, completely terrifying her, the car shot backwards and hit a sports car.

Panicking, she moved the gear thing again until the car stopped moving and hit the button to make the engine stop. Leah started to cry, thinking that she was in trouble and would probably not get any pocket money until she was about twenty years old, like the time she knocked a glass ornament over in a shop and her mum had to pay for it.

Then it dawned on her that she wasn't going to get in trouble, because there was nobody left to tell her off.

Crying harder, she curled up on the back seat, where she eventually realised she was cold. Resigned, she turned the fan to hot, shut the door, and lay down to cry some more.

SHOPPING

"Morning, old bean!" shouted Neil from outside Dan's caravan, banging on the hatefully thin wall. He groaned inside his sleeping bag. Bad idea to have finished the whole bottle of single malt, but the apocalypse waited for no man. Dan struggled out of bed and stumbled outside.

Neil already had the camp cooker going and had rescued bacon to go with the eggs. Deciding that some greasy food was definitely the way forward, Dan drank water from a bottle and clumsily retrieved his toothbrush to try and get the feel of dead cats out of his mouth.

"Morning, happy," croaked Dan. "Keep the noise down, please?"

"If you say so, boss!" he replied, loud as ever. "Today, we're going to have a look around locally. There's an industrial estate over there," he said, pointing past the petrol station. "I'm going to find what I can. You coming, lightweight?"

Neil stood there with a grin, waiting for his baited hook to catch Dan's cheek.

Dan refused to be goaded and mildly agreed that the idea was a good one. Visibly disappointed, Neil raised his voice louder and adopted a new character, that of the USMC Drill Sergeant from *Full Metal Jacket*. Before the repertoire got too loud for Dan, he held a hand up to stop the tirade.

"OK, mate, take a minute and we'll set off after breakfast," Neil said, relenting.

Over their bacon and eggs, Neil listed what he wanted to find. "We need a pump to get all that diesel from the petrol station, and either a tanker or plenty of cans to put it in. I want to find a seven-and-a-half-ton truck to load up with the longer-lasting stuff, because it stinks in there and I don't want to have to suffer that every time you sleep in and I have to fetch my own breakfast…"

That got a warning eyebrow raised by Dan, but nothing said.

"We need tools, vehicle tools too. Or at least know where to get them, and a couple of saws; we can't be faffing about like you do for ten minutes opening a door," he continued, slightly more softly this time. "We need more spray paint so people know where to find us too."

Dan agreed, and they set off for the industrial estate in one Land Rover, after moving nearly all the kit to the caravans. They found a car garage that contained all the tools Neil needed, and he reckoned he could even get the tyre machines working with a generator. Definitely one to note for the future.

Dan perked up when they found a small unit marked "Shooting Supplies." The doors took some beating, but eventually they were in. The teenage boy in both of them came out, and a large selection of knives was added to the shopping list. They selected a decent folding knife and a fixed blade each and attached them to themselves, looking ever more the Mad Max characters. Neil still had his Glock in the back of his waistband, not being able to bring himself to wear the "poser" leg holster like Dan did.

Handguns being what they were in Britain – highly bloody illegal – no alternative holsters were readily available for Neil's weapon. Dan made a note to hit an army surplus soon and get some kit for them both.

Not knowing what the future would hold, they took an armful of twelve-bore shotguns, six boxes of cartridges, and Dan insisted on a crossbow and a competition bow. "Ammo will run out one day, and on that day, you'll be glad you know Robin Hood here, unless you want to be vegetarian," teased Dan.

Before they left, Dan stopped and stared at something under the glass counter. Neil went over and saw that he was looking at a two-foot-long curved machete, like a cross between a kukri and a broadsword. Dan helped himself to it and fixed Neil in a serious stare.

"You don't think zombies will…" he started.

Neil stared back at him for a long time. "Nah. No chance, that's just films, mate," and then he helped himself to a similar tool as they left.

Neil found the truck he wanted to start loading with supplies: hard sides and a working tail lift. It started easily enough, after they broke into the unit and luckily found the keys on a hook and not in the pockets of one of the bodies there.

They hit the builder's merchants and got two large two-stroke disc cutters with spare blades – much quicker at opening doors than a key – and some petrol cans to fill up later. Neil went off to find the stuff he wanted for the fuel pump, muttering to himself and seemingly working it out on his hands as he went, which left Dan free to wander around. He found three petrol generators and went to retrieve them. After trying to lift the first, he decided it would be better to wait for Neil.

They loaded the three generators, with difficulty, and the other stuff into the truck and headed back to the supermarket. Neil had a plan for pumping out the fuel into jerrycans, which he'd got about twenty of, which should give them weeks of fuel. He said he still wanted a fuel tanker – just a little one – and that Dan should keep his eyes open.

He seemed to be busy sorting the fuel side, so Dan said he was going to head out past the Land Rover garage because he knew of a specialist 4x4 place where he hoped he could find some of the good stuff for the Defenders. They agreed what to do if Dan didn't return by dark: Neil would try the radio, and if nothing happened, he would set off to the garage at first light and try to find him.

Dan checked his gun's chamber, reassuring himself with the glint of brass he could see, climbed into his Land Rover, and called out to Neil, "Just keep an eye out; not everyone may be as friendly as me."

PENNY

Her feet hurt. She wasn't used to walking and didn't own any hard-wearing boots or appropriate trousers. She'd settled on flat shoes instead of her normal small heels and was already in pain. A teacher for more than twenty years, and she had become soft. Penny was not happy with this turn of events. Her car had been blocked in by a crashed van in the road where she lived, and it simply did not occur to her to steal a replacement, let alone move the dead driver of the van. She had called 999 only to get a dead tone until the phone lines went down completely.

She still thought of taking a vehicle as looting or theft, not survival. To her, these were still the possessions of other people and should be respected as such. She'd stayed at home for as long as she could bear, waiting for the authorities to give direction.

As she walked, she reasoned with herself that she really had to find something to eat, and a way of getting home to sleep that night preferably without walking. A faint sound permeated her thoughts; it sounded like a lawnmower being started, and she found that distinctly strange. Why would anyone not affected by whatever this was be cutting their grass at a time like this?

She decided to walk towards the sound and ask the unlikely gardener precisely what they were doing.

It took a long time, but by following the sounds, she could make out the clear tone of an engine running. Rounding a bend on the footpath, she found the source of the noise to be coming from a petrol station, but it wasn't coming from a car. She was startled to see a man fighting with some hosepipes and other items that he was trying to fit on what looked like a generator.

Penny straightened herself, attempted to make herself more respectable by running her hands through her hair, and made a confident approach to the man. He did not hear or see her coming, as he was engrossed in his task, and he jumped in fright when she called "Hello" to him.

The man stood there panting with a hand on his chest for a few beats and the other behind his back until he took a deep breath and drew himself up.

"Hi there, I'm Neil. Are you OK?" he said while reaching for a bottle of water that he handed to her.

"P-P-Penny. Thank you," she stammered, accepting the water before she straightened and replied far more confidently.

"I'm Penny. I can't say how glad I am to see another person who isn't…" She trailed off; the words were too difficult to say yet.

She walked towards Neil and extended her hand, which he shook. She opened her mouth to speak, but didn't know what to say. Tears threatened to overcome her, so she quickly closed her mouth. Neil switched off the generator and invited her to come back to where they had set up camp.

Penny followed autonomously, until it dawned on her what Neil had said.

"We?" she asked hopefully.

"Yes," said Neil. "My mate Dan is off shopping at the moment, but he should be back soon. Do you want any food? Drink?" As he turned, Penny saw the clear outline of a gun under his T-shirt where it was tucked in the small of his back.

She instinctively stopped, unsure whether to question or challenge this new discovery. She decided that in good conscience, she must ask him about it.

"Neil, may I please ask if you are armed?" she said properly.

"Yeah, we just don't know who is friendly and who isn't. Don't worry about it, honestly."

It was as much explanation as she expected, really. She decided that she probably needed people like these men nowadays, and she shouldn't be squeamish.

"It's OK. I apologise for my tone. I'm just not used to these things, you see?"

Neil said he understood. He went into one of the two caravans and came out with a bag and arms full. He put the things into the back of a big car, started a camping cooker, and poured water into an old-style tin kettle. He told her the story of how he met Dan two days ago, and how they came to be where they were. He told her about his wife and boys, how he spent a day digging in the garden to bury them before making his way. He said this all in a flat tone, staring off into space. When he finished, he shook the sensations away and forced a smile. In a broad Belfast accent, he asked, "Noy, Penny, can aye get you a cup of tea?"

WOMEN AND CHILDREN

Dan pushed the Defender hard on the way back south, testing its limits and capabilities long before he had to find out the hard way. He drove systematically, clinically, like he'd been taught to for so many years.

He passed the Land Rover garage they'd visited the day before and glanced in as he passed at speed. He pushed on until he reached the place he wanted. One look at the building and he knew this wouldn't be easy to get into; all the windows were barred, the rear gates were solid and high, and the whole shop front had heavy horizontal anti-ram barriers. A quick assessment looking for the least resistant way in, and he stopped. Out loud, he said to himself, "Fuck it; it's not like I'm paying for the damage."

The heavy chain he'd picked up and attached to the rear bumper was looped onto the bars of the front door. The Defender's torque didn't struggle at all to rip the doors out, leaving the horizontal bar in place. He looped the chain back onto the spare wheel on the back door of the Rover and climbed inside.

Over the next half hour, he posted out the things he wanted – more speed jacks and tow ropes and a set of five big off-road wheels and tyres, completely filling the boot space – before having a good look around the warehouse in the back. Dan made a mental note to use Defenders and clear the place out ASAP. Neil would need a well-equipped garage, but he could keep a few Land Rovers going for years with this stuff.

After trying to cover up the worst of the damage to the door, he made his way back towards "base camp," this time at a little more of a relaxed pace.

He passed the Land Rover garage again, but this time he thought that something wasn't right. As soon as it dawned on him, he slammed on the brakes, causing his new looted kit to crash around. He slammed into reverse and backed up at speed, skidding again to a stop in front of the garage.

Where the daytime lights of the X5 were shining straight at him.

He got out and drew the gun, holding it behind his right leg. Creeping over the smashed glass, he called out, "Hello? Is anyone there?"

A glance inside the BMW showed rubbish and empty bottles on the back seat, like someone had been sleeping in the car. A sound made him turn, and he saw a young girl frozen in fear with headphones in her ears and a biscuit halfway towards her open mouth.

Dan turned his left shoulder slowly forward, hiding the gun behind his back. "It's OK. I'm not going to hurt you, I promise," he tried. She didn't move other than to swallow hard and stare at him. "I'm Dan. You were here yesterday, weren't you? You ran away."

The girl stayed still for a while longer before popping the biscuit into her mouth and chewing fast and removing her headphones.

"I'm Leah," she said.

"Hi, Leah. How old are you?"

"Twe… Fifteen," she lied unconvincingly. "Why do you have a gun?"

Dan slowly holstered the sidearm and held both hands up to her, palms out.

"It's to protect me and my friend. He has one too. You saw him yesterday."

"OK," she replied. "I tried to drive your car to Morrisons but I crashed it backwards. Sorry."

Dan laughed. "It's all right, I didn't really like it anyway! Too flash for me!" He studied her carefully before he decided how to word the next sentence. "Look, I know you aren't supposed to go anywhere with people you don't know, but I'd like it if you would come back to our camp so you're safe and protected. I really think it's best. We have hot food and you'd have your own brand-new caravan to sleep in, which you can lock with your own keys if you want."

Leah studied him with her head slightly cocked. "For a minute there, I thought you were going to try and offer me sweets," she replied with an uncertain smirk.

Dan was taken aback slightly that she had given him sarcasm already. "I'm not one of those people. I've got…" He trailed off, eyes suddenly glazing over before he tried again. "There are people out there who wouldn't be kind to you, but we're not those people."

Leah thought about it for a while longer before nodding.

Dan told her, "Jump in then," and he climbed into the driver's seat. He was very wary not to seem like he was fussing over her too much; caring instincts might come across wrong to her at the moment, so he decided to treat her like she was a bit older than she looked.

Leah just looked out of the window on the way back. Dan drove carefully and just kept the uncomfortable silence. He decided that he'd have to make a trip to get her more appropriate clothes. Maybe later, or tomorrow.

He pulled back into the car park, passing the fuel station where he expected Neil to be. The generator looked abandoned and the pipes were a mess. He hadn't cut the top off the reservoir tank yet. It looked wrong.

Accelerating towards the caravans, he feared the worst, but as he came to a halt in front of their makeshift cooking area, he was speechless to find Neil sitting drinking tea with a woman he guessed was a little older than him.

They, in turn, looked equally shocked to see Dan return at speed with a confused young girl sitting in the passenger's seat.

Then there were four.

MORE SHOPPING

"It seems some introductions are in order," said the woman as she stood and smoothed her clothes.

"I'm Penny. Pleased to meet you, Daniel."

Dan shook the offered hand, dumbstruck.

"And who is this young lady?" she asked, bending down to Leah with a smile.

"I'm Leah," she replied, returning the smile.

"How did you…" Dan said.

"Oh, I was just wandering around until I scared Neil here half to death!"

Neil stood there smiling and offered a guilty shrug.

Dan recovered slightly and turned to Leah. "Looks like you won't have that caravan all to yourself after all."

"I don't mind," Leah said, still smiling.

Dan shook himself out of the shock of suddenly having two more mouths to feed, and a woman and child to protect at that. "Right then, ladies, I think we need to take you both shopping. You'll both need new clothes and sleeping bags."

Neil offered to stay and cook dinner while they went. All agreed, and Dan started to clear out the scavenged stuff from his Defender. Neil bagged a speed jack and Dan told him that where he'd been would definitely need clearing out to equip the garage he'd have when they got permanently settled.

Dan drove them to the camping shop where he and Neil had spent a night and started collecting more wind-up lamps and other tools while Penny breezed through the shop selecting items for her and Leah. After ten minutes, they both had a few sets of clothes packed into their new backpacks and a pair of walking boots. Dan suggested they get a good, warm waterproof each, which they did. They took an armful of sleeping bags to boot, which seemed sensible because of the rate they were gathering survivors, and loaded the Land Rover.

Penny saw another shop and asked Dan very formally if he would kindly open the doors for them and give them both a minute. The large pry bar got the sliding doors to a small Primark open quickly, and he asked them to stay outside just while he checked it was OK; he didn't want either of them to trip over a body. He couldn't smell anything as he walked through the shop, gun in hand. He grabbed a few packs of boxer shorts and socks for him and Neil and returned outside.

"I'll be out here, ladies. Take as long as you need," he said.

They went inside. They clearly needed underwear too, but they weren't exactly well acquainted enough to discuss it openly yet.

Dan lit up and kept an eye up and down the high street. He was finishing his second smoke by the time they reappeared, bags in hand and carrying some pillows.

"I took the liberty of getting a pillow each for you two," said Penny.

"Thank you," he replied. "Do you need to go anywhere else?"

They didn't. By the time they got back to camp, Neil had set up more camping chairs and erected a gazebo over the cooking area. Very cosy.

They sat around, waiting for whatever Neil was cooking to be ready, and discussed the plans for the next day. Thankfully, Penny seemed to be a natural planner; she suggested that Neil and Dan would go out and "shop" again – she still couldn't use words like *scavenge* and *survivors* – while she and Leah stayed there and started to sort out bringing the food out of Morrisons and loading the lorry.

They talked about plans and ideas for a while. Leah sat and listened until she stifled the third yawn in a row. Penny packed her off to bed after making her do her teeth with her new toothbrush and went in the female caravan for a while to settle her.

Penny came back out and sat down with a sigh. By this point, Neil had produced the Scotch and poured two; Penny raised an eyebrow at him until he poured a third.

"That poor girl. She must be very confused about all this, and we must shelter her from these horrors for as long as possible."

"Penny," said Neil hesitantly, changing the subject. "Have you ever used a gun?"

Penny chuckled and said that she'd done clay-pigeon shooting before. She then said, "So you may as well leave me one of those shotguns and a box of cartridges when you go tomorrow. I won't need it, but it's probably sensible to leave it here."

They agreed and sat in silence for a while before their emerging matriarch dismissed them to bed, as they had an early start.

BAD PEOPLE

Kev got up like normal in his clockwork life. His mum wasn't up already, which was strange. He was used to her waking him up for breakfast before he went to work, but she had gone to bed early and he'd fallen asleep to the sound of her coughing.

He tried to wake her up, but she was still and cold. He put an extra blanket over her and left her to rest, just like she did when he was poorly.

He was hungry, but he was going to be late for work if he didn't go soon. He liked his routine; it gave him purpose, and every day ran like clockwork for him. He got dressed, got his bike from the hallway of their small maisonette, and locked the front door before he cycled off to work.

He got to the industrial area where the factory was after ten minutes. Kev hadn't noticed that there was nobody around; his brain didn't work like that.

Nobody was at the factory, which wasn't right. Kev didn't like it when things weren't right, and he was scared. Two people walked along the road drinking from glass bottles; they saw him sitting there and started to shout at him.

People being nasty to Kev was something he was used to, so he did what he always did and turned his face away, screwing his eyes shut to ignore them. They stood in front of where he was sitting and shouted, but he wouldn't answer them. One of them picked his bike up, and when Kev looked at him with his temper rising, they laughed. They threw his bike over the railings where it landed in the small rubbish-filled brook.

Kev jumped to his feet and let out an angry keening noise. When they saw his size – well over six feet tall and very heavily built – they ran away, laughing.

Kev sat down again. He was scared, he was angry, and he started to cry. He sat there all day, not wanting to miss his shift. He didn't have a watch because he couldn't tell the time very well. His clockwork life was in complete turmoil, and he stayed there all night.

The next morning, cold and terrified, Jimmy found him. He liked Jimmy, who told him that he would look after him now.

GETTING ORGANISED

Dan woke early to the sound of Neil getting dressed. He followed suit and both walked a respectable distance along the side of the store to relieve themselves.

Neil's plan was to finish clearing the industrial estate nearby, and he wanted to get the fuel pump going so they had a ready supply of diesel. If they were going to have to go further afield to scavenge, they'd need to be carrying plenty of fuel. He decided they should also have a few mobile battery packs for starting cars, and said that they should recover more Defenders like the ones they had. They both agreed to bring back an extra caravan each that day, hoping for more people to fill them.

The spare weapons were hidden away in their caravan under the lounge settees, apart from the shotgun Penny selected. They emptied their Land Rovers and checked them over. Each packed a bag of food and water, and put a lightweight sleeping bag in just in case. Another large breakfast of bacon and eggs was produced – Penny cooked, telling them that they should eat up before it spoiled. She was already putting things into cool boxes and getting very organised. Leah was still asleep.

Neil and Dan shook hands and wished each other luck. They again agreed on what messages they would leave on key buildings that would attract other survivors.

Dan set off towards the nearest big town, about a ten-mile drive. He went slowly, looking for any signs of life. He still had the Glock, but had a .22 rifle on the dash in front of him. Nothing spectacular: eight-round magazine bolt-action, but it had a good optic on it. They had both taken a local A-Z and had decided to mark sites that needed properly clearing in the future. Dan stopped and made a note about a small shop with a pharmacy. Medicines would become very important soon. To minimise the risk of infections, which wouldn't have been an issue last week, they decided to wear gloves and use hand sanitiser. Gas masks were to be worn when moving bodies too.

He took the smaller roads, as he thought he wouldn't see much from the dual track. He stopped by a large pub and used spray paint to write a message on the wall directing survivors to the Morrisons base camp.

As he climbed back in, he saw a sign to Her Majesty's Prison Manor Grange. The thought of bodies rotting in their cells, never to be released, was a grim one.

He continued to the town centre, marking the locations of another two shops worth visiting when they had more hands to help. He saw movement by some houses and stopped to paint another message on the side, not wanting a repeat and scaring someone like he did with Leah. Softly, softly, catchee monkey.

He marked another industrial estate, and as he drove slowly through, he saw a man siphoning fuel from a van. The man straightened when he heard the engine, and he stood up tall with a crowbar in his right hand. He was huge. Taller than Dan and outweighing him.

Dan pulled up well short of the big man, and got out slowly. The man said nothing, and Dan broke the silence.

"Hi," he said, getting no reply. "We're gathering survivors together. There are four of us already and we have a plan. Come with us?"

The man still said nothing and stood still. A flicker of his eyes over Dan's shoulder and the slightest crunch of gravel made him spin and draw the Glock. A younger man had crept dangerously close behind him carrying another crowbar. He panicked and dropped it straight away, holding both hands up.

"Whoa! Whoa! Don't shoot me! Fuck! Sorry…sorry, it's just that Kev here doesn't trust people any more. Not after they nicked his bike."

The younger man still cowered, backing away and shaking. A quick glance at Kev showed that he hadn't moved an inch. He assessed them both: Kev was about thirty and huge. Shaved head, dull eyes. The younger one was probably early twenties. Lean but with an intelligence and clearly some stealth, as he'd got way too close to Dan undetected.

He made a judgement call and holstered the gun, although he was sure to keep his hand close by it.

"Sorry, boys, bit jumpy myself. Kev, you want to put that down, mate?"

Kev just looked at the other guy, who walked over to him and spoke like he was talking to a child. "It's OK, Kev, he's not bad like the others."

Kev didn't speak; he just looked at the other man with a questioning, almost pleading face.

The younger man looked at Dan, not entirely convinced himself, and said, "Yeah, mate, he won't hurt you."

Dan went to the Defender and retrieved a thermos full of coffee. "Brew, lads?" he asked. Always a deal-maker.

As they stood by the front of the Land Rover, Dan offered out the fags. Jimmy took one; Kev just shook his head and looked at the floor. He told them the brief version of their story and asked Kev and Jimmy what had happened to them.

"We work in one of the factories here. Known Kev for ages; he's a big lump but wouldn't hurt a fly." In a hushed voice, he added, "Kev had the cord around his neck when he was born. He's a bit slow, but he's a good lad, really."

Kev heard anyway and smiled at what he took as a compliment.

Jimmy continued, "Kev got up and rode his bike to work like normal. I found him here sitting on the floor, and it looks like someone knocked him down and took his bike. They just threw it over the fence for no reason. Bastards. We've been trying to put some supplies together, and that's what we were doing when you drove up."

Dan told them again that he wanted them to join the group. He offered them food, company, and their own caravan. He told them that he needed their help to collect enough supplies and survivors and find somewhere permanent to live.

Jimmy liked the idea, and asked Kev if he wanted to go and meet Dan's friends. Kev smiled and nodded. He drove them to the van they'd started to load and saw another 7.5-ton truck similar to the one they already had back at camp.

Dan got to show off some burglary skills getting into the unit, where the keys were still on the desk. Jimmy used the fuel they'd collected to fill it up, and they began moving their supplies into the bigger vehicle. Dan saw they had a portable generator, and when Kev went to pick it up, Dan started to speak to warn him so he didn't hurt himself. Before he'd managed a word, Kev braced himself and heaved it up. Impressive – those things were one hundred kilos plus.

Jimmy and Kev started their new ride and followed Dan on the drive. At the next stop, instead of marking the little pharmacy they saw, all three loaded everything into boxes and into the truck in about half an hour.

Dan stopped periodically to paint the message for other survivors. They didn't see anyone else that day, and after the long way round and many stops to spread the good word, they found themselves back at the caravan sales pitch. Dan got out and lit a fag, offering one to Jimmy by habit.

"Kev, want to pick your caravan?"

Kev looked at Jimmy, who nodded to him. He was delighted and skipped off to look at them. Dan reckoned the acquired brain injury had left Kev like a six-foot-four, nineteen-stone five-year-old who didn't speak. For a while, he utterly envied him, as ignorance would have been bliss right now.

Kev eventually chose one, bouncing on the spot and pointing. It got hitched to the Land Rover and they set off again, slowly this time, as Dan's towing experience had only started in this very spot a couple of days ago.

As there was still a lot of daylight left, Dan asked Jimmy if they wouldn't mind staying out for a few more hours until their truck was full.

Jimmy agreed and spoke to Kev. "Still got some graft left, Kev?" Kev just smiled and nodded. Jimmy acted like the little big brother to him. It turned out that Kev had worked in the factory since he was sixteen. Jimmy had left school at the same age without much in the way of prospects, but after the rounds of working as a labourer for a few years, he found himself on the line next to Kev, until he was made foreman before too long. Jimmy had a kind of sharp intelligence, not in the way of an educated man but something far more useful. He was switched on, savvy, cunning, but kind. "The thing with Kev is, he doesn't know to do stuff by himself mostly. Tell him what to do and he won't rest until it's done, but he'd just starve to death if he were on his own because nobody would cook for him or remind him to eat. He was in a mess when I found him; sat outside work cold and hungry. He'd waited all night for the doors to open and I found him the next day. He's strong as an ox but gentle with it. Not a bad bone in his body."

They helped themselves to crisps and drinks at a garage, again emptying the shelves of long-dated foodstuff, plus all the cigarettes and alcohol, before loading up and setting off again. They found a DIY shop and Dan marked it on his map while Jimmy and Kev broke in. They came back with some fuel cans and a circular concrete saw – Jimmy's idea of a key in the new world.

"Great minds," Dan said. "We got two of those yesterday!"

Dan spent some time looking at the A-Z over a coffee and a smoke, cooking some ideas, while Jimmy started with the spray paint. Jimmy left a message on the shop and then started to daub something on the truck.

Intrigued, Dan walked over to look. On the side of their small lorry, Jimmy had painted "Survivor camp, join today for free – ask driver for details" in some grim parody of a breakdown service.

With a smile, Dan said they should probably head back. As they drove into the car park, they could see another caravan already in place. The pump at the petrol station seemed to have been finished, and all the empty fuel cans were gone.

As they pulled up, he was happy to see another face he didn't yet know standing nervously by Penny. He was glad that she was turning out to be a kind of mother hen figure. He had a plan to build a kind of society for as many people as they could find, but he couldn't do what he wanted to do – go and find those survivors – if he was stuck at base camp organising everything.

Penny wasted no time in welcoming the new members. Dan introduced Kev and Jimmy and gave a quick rundown of how he met them, adding under his breath that Kev had an acquired brain injury.

"James. Kevin," she said formally, offering a hand to both in turn. "Pleasure to have you with us." She gently grilled Jimmy about their history and skills, quickly figuring that the addition of two physically capable men was a plus. They went into their new caravan, which was being set up by Neil, to stow their new gear and look around what was now home.

She in turn introduced their own recruit. The new person was called Andrew and was very usefully an accountant. He was tall and thin, with a permanently worried expression. Dan quickly realised that he didn't have much of a clue when it came to life without modern comforts, but every extra pair of hands was a godsend to their cause and every surviving human being was a miracle.

Penny hadn't been idle; a healthy stack of supplies was loaded into Neil's 7.5 tonner and organised well. Andrew had wandered up to them not long after Dan and Neil had left, and after a small induction was put to work emptying the shop. Leah had helped under Penny's direction, and she smiled at Dan when she saw him. *God only knows what is going through her head*, he thought.

He walked away with Neil to the fuel pumps nominally to look over what he'd done, but more to discuss their new recruits. Neil had managed to pump out nearly two hundred litres of diesel – plenty for what they needed in the short term, but he still wanted a fuel tanker if they saw one.

"Andrew's a bit of a wet lettuce, but he seems nice enough," Neil said quietly. "Doesn't have much of an idea what to do, but Penny's been working him hard all day!"

Dan smiled. "Already we're in a matriarchal society, and I thought things might be different now…" They both chuckled, and then trailed off into silence, thinking of their own matriarchs of last week, no longer with them.

A meal on the camp stoves, all seven of them quiet in their own thoughts, made Dan think that cooking for a group any larger would take full-time organising. He made a mental note to rescue a commercial chef at the first opportunity.

They turned in: Dan and Neil to their caravan, Penny and Leah to theirs, Jimmy and Kev to one of the new additions to the circus, and Andrew on his own.

Then there were seven.

NEW WORLD ORDER

Breakfast was early; Penny saw to that as she started cooking the eggs and bacon, singing what sounded like hymns.

One by one, the survivors came out into the world. When they were all gathered, Penny cleared her throat and called for everyone's attention. "Good morning, everyone." She paused. Dan wasn't sure if they were expected to chorus "good morning" back to her.

"I have drawn up plans for today. I hope you don't mind me taking the liberty." She paused again, scanning the group. On hearing and seeing no exceptions raised, she continued with confidence. "Sit, everyone, please," she fussed. "Now, our immediate supply issues are well catered for, as the contents of this supermarket will sustain us for many months. However, we have further considerations if we intend to spend the coming winter in any form of comfort… Daniel here has set us all on a path, to some extent. It's fair to say that many of us would be wandering without much in the way of purpose had this man not sought to bring us together for a common cause."

Dan realised that Penny was clearly used to public speaking, even if she did have a tendency to address the group as though they were children in her school. He was half expecting a flip chart to be produced at any moment.

"Our long-term survival depends on our ability to seek out more survivors and create a society that can be sustained in the future without the modern comforts we are all accustomed to." Leah and

Kev had already lost track of the speech entirely but seemed glued to Penny's words anyway, waiting to hear their names. Penny glanced at Dan, who got a sense that she was asking his permission to proceed. He gave a subtle nod as he bent his head to his black coffee, encouraging her to press on.

"Our priority is to find others like us, but the problem in doing so is that we may quickly overrun ourselves with mouths to feed, so to speak. To that end, and in anticipation of further additions, I have tasked everyone as follows…" Nobody argued, not that they had a choice as Penny went on with her tasking. "James and Kevin, you two are now our chief recovery agents. You are to empty your vehicle and collect the supplies marked by Daniel on his map. I have prioritised these and listed them for you. I am assured that you know how to use the new equipment to enter these premises?" She referred to the circular cutting saw recovered yesterday.

"No problem," said Jimmy. "Me and Kev will have it all back here ready for tea," he added with a smile.

"Wonderful," said Penny. "Neil, with your expertise, might I suggest that you be named our Head of Engineering? Your impressive display with the petrol solution and previous experience make you the ideal candidate." She carried on, without waiting for agreement, which Dan could tell annoyed Neil. Not because Neil had any objection, but because Dan knew him well enough already to recognise when he was going to quote a film in a perfect mimic of the actor.

"I'd like you to take Andrew with you today, and collect another caravan from the place you found. With instruction, he should be able to bring it back here in preparation. Another vehicle for him would be in order too. After that, if you could return and continue your search of the industrial area as discussed?"

Neil nodded, raising his coffee in salute.

"Andrew, after collecting a vehicle and caravan with Neil and being shown how to arrange it properly, I would be grateful if you would continue to recover and load supplies from the supermarket into our lorry here," she said, indicating Neil's truck.

Andrew agreed. Dan thought he didn't seem the type of person to disagree much.

"Daniel," Penny moved on, fixing him with a look, a look that almost pleaded for support, as if only he and she knew how very important it was to establish a hierarchy this early and to have an unchallenged leadership, "if you could kindly continue your search of the area, mark buildings that you wish James and Kevin to empty for the group, and focus your attention towards finding us a permanent site?"

Dan paused. He was genuinely happy that Penny was taking the lead, as he simply didn't have the patience with people to do this kind of thing every day, but he didn't think it wise to fold immediately to instruction and be seen as just one of the pawns of the group. He needed to retain or establish a kind of leadership role to the others, the better for making decisions that they would need to listen to if push came to shove. He didn't want to ride roughshod over Penny's newly accepted social leadership, so this needed to be worded carefully.

"Good plan, Penny, but Jimmy and Kev have enough locally to be getting on with. I need to make a trip to gather some sensitive supplies that are key to our future. I may be away overnight." He left it there, with a heavy hint of something secret.

"I'll resume my scouting locally after this, unless there are any objections?" Nobody had any.

"Very well. I shall stay here, prepare food for later, and assist in the disposal of the spoiled goods."

Dan noticed that she had deliberately given herself a job that would turn most people's stomachs. *Clever move.* He reminded himself to offer Penny a gas mask before he went.

She continued, "We all have our jobs to do, shall we continue within the hour?"

Everyone went to get up when Leah said, "What about me?"

That stopped everyone where they were, and Penny said, "You will stay here and assist me." She went to leave, and everyone took his or her cues from her.

"I want to help Dan," Leah said.

An air of awkwardness shadowed the group. Penny didn't know how to squash Leah's ambition without hurting her feelings and embarrassing her publicly.

"Leah, how about you come with me after I'm back?" said Dan, trying to rescue the situation from the possibility of a teenage strop.

Leah thought about this for a few seconds before saying, with a beaming smile, "OK, but you promised, so you have to take me."

That seemed fair.

Penny came to find Dan a short time later, and saw him in conversation with Neil. "Gentlemen, I do hope you don't think me too forward?" she asked hopefully.

"Not at all, Penny," said Dan. "We were just saying how glad we are that you are taking control; we need your organisational skills to keep this group together and moving with a purpose. I didn't want to say in front of everyone, but I'm going to an army camp I know, and it's a couple of hours away at least. To do this properly, I'll need time to recce the area and make sure it's safe."

Both Penny and Neil started to raise objections simultaneously, but Dan held up his hands.

"Trust me, I'm capable. And I'm going to be very careful," Dan reasoned. "We need to be aware that people may want to take what we have, and until we are strong enough as a group, then we need to consider some kind of guard. I'd like Neil to stay home for now, unless we find someone able to protect the camp when I'm away. In the interim, I don't want him far from the camp. If someone turns up again like Andrew did, then I want you two," he pointed at Neil and Penny in turn, "to stay in radio contact using the walkie-talkies. If you can't get him, Penny, blast the horn on the truck and he'll come back."

Neil had already run through this with Dan before Penny showed up, and he nodded his agreement to her.

"Very well, that seems sensible. However, I want you to think of excuses for not taking Leah with you. I don't want her seeing things that she shouldn't."

Dan wanted to say that Leah had already seen things that no young girl should have to see, but he gently deferred that conversation.

Neil again tried to reason with Dan that he should come with him, but he flatly refused. "If we're both away until tomorrow night, there's no way of knowing that we would come back to anyone here. It's too risky to have us both leave. Face it, until we get more people here we can trust to protect the camp, then you have to stay here or very nearby. End of."

No objections. Penny deftly changed the subject.

"As we recruit more, we won't be able to give everyone jobs over breakfast. We need to have departmental heads and delegate as we see fit. As Chief Engineer and First Ranger, I expect you to consider this seriously."

First Ranger, thought Dan. Well, that job title didn't work out well in *Game of Thrones*, did it? A glance at Neil told him that he would have to suffer some film-referenced jokes and impressions after he had been dubbed that.

He stayed where he was and lit a smoke as the other two walked back, talking. Dan wanted the group to be protected and organised. At the same time, he craved some solitude.

He finished his smoke and went to his Defender. He topped off the tank, loaded two extra jerrycans, and checked his equipment. He took extra food and water – obviously, there would be plenty of places to loot on the way – a camp cooker, and his sleeping bag. Sleeping in the back of a Land Rover didn't qualify as a hardship to Dan. His dad used to call it a "night in the Mootel." Farming joke.

As he went to set off, he found Leah standing by his car door. She seemed to want to say something, but just stood there.

"I'll be back tomorrow," he said.

"Promise?" she asked, her eyes full of innocence.

Dan was raised never to make a promise he couldn't keep, and there were just too many variables. "I said I'd take you out on a trip. You can be Second Ranger as soon as I can make it happen." That would have to do.

"What did you used to be?" she asked, surprising him.

"Tell you what," Dan replied, "when you can figure it out, I'll take you with me." She frowned at him, clearly thinking this was unfair, but he drove away before she could say anything else.

"Take care beyond the wall, Stark," Neil called solemnly as Dan drove past.

"Knob," replied Dan with a smile, leaving the camp behind. He felt better. Better to be out on his own, unburdened by the responsibility of protecting them even for a short time, but more confident that they would be safe without him.

GETTING OUTSOLDIERED

Dan moved along the roads steadily and with confidence as he had driven them many times before. He passed bodies, days-old car crashes, and even evidence of a house fire. Not a sign of anybody. He didn't stop to paint the messages he had the day before; he had a purpose, a goal, and he needed a plan to do this safely. The payday he was after was serious. Military armouries were likely to be far more popular than a Morrisons, and would probably be defended if anyone was still alive around there.

As he drove, he thought of the society that Penny envisaged based on the thoughts they shared. He was obviously marked as the head of operations.

Ops Commander, Dan: First Ranger – it sounded a little too grand for his liking. He had a Society Leader: Head of Base Camp in Penny. She could assess new recruits and set work tasks, keep everyone busy.

Head of Engineering was now Neil, although he wasn't really interested in a leadership role, it seemed. Maybe he could get Neil to teach some of the younger ones in the future. Maybe some science geeks survived, and they could work out things like manufacturing biodiesel and using solar panels to heat water.

Scavenging teams needed to be beefed up; Dan liked Jimmy and Kev, but he just needed more like them.

He needed to find farmers, people who could grow crops as well as rear animals. He needed animals, for that matter. He needed people who knew how to cut down trees for firewood, people who knew how to hunt and fish – not just for now, but to teach people in the future. Dan could teach the basics of shooting and fishing, but he already had too little time.

He needed to find people who could cook large meals from limited supplies. He needed people with medical expertise, as his own training was good for first aid and bullet wounds. A surgeon would be good.

He needed to find people with skills like his own; what good was a First Ranger without other Rangers?

So many mental notes were made that he had to stop for a break and make actual ones. Coffee and smoke time. There was a time not too long ago, five days in fact, when he called that breakfast.

The more he thought about it, the more rabbit holes he fell down. He would need hundreds of people with a range of experience and expertise to get this easy idea of a new society going. It seemed an impossible task at the time, so he tried to push it all from his mind and concentrate on the immediate.

Go and get some serious weaponry – three clips for a Glock and a small-calibre rifle weren't going to protect much. After that, worry about recruitment and training.

He thought about where they were going to set up this utopian cooperative society. He had an idea forming but this would require an in-depth local recce when he was back at camp, and probably a lot more bodies to make it happen.

OK, maybe *bodies* wasn't the best choice of words.

He arrived in the area of the camp after three hours, and decided to scout around slowly. He marked a huge camping store on his map for a priority clearance sale, and doubted whether Jimmy and Kev could fit it all in one truck – maybe a group outing soon?

He parked well away from the base and walked a long way round to approach it from higher ground. He'd brought a small rucksack of gear and the hard-wearing waterproof sleeping bag with him. He didn't think it was going to rain, but realised it had been years since he had really studied the weather and not checked a forecast app.

Damn technology – it had made him soft and lazy.

He settled in, watching the base from the scope, at around four in the afternoon. He figured that if he watched from now until daybreak and saw nobody, then the camp was safe to approach.

Just as the sun dropped behind him, he reconsidered waiting through the night. There was no sign of movement at all, and the place definitely looked deserted. He could clearly make out the shape of the now deceased Ministry of Defence police officer in the small booth on the closed gate, and was impatient to get more in the way of munitions.

He shuffled back from the small ridge, collected his gear, and slung his rifle on his back. He decided to use the last of the light to get into the base.

Too many thoughts must have been going through his head. He was complacent. Lazy. Foolish to have insisted he went alone.

"Stop right there, laddie," called a gravelly Scottish voice from nowhere, heavily punctuated by the sound of a large round being chambered. "Guns on the ground and I'll be knowing your business here."

"OK, let's just take it easy," said Dan slowly as he held the rifle away from his body by the barrel with his left hand and lowered his body. This was intentional, as it freed the right hand to be near the gun holstered on his right leg. He couldn't see the owner of the voice and thought that there may still be a chance to get the drop on him.

That idea was quickly crushed when the man appeared behind his right shoulder. "Don't. Finger and thumb, on the ground."

Dan slowly removed his sidearm using only his thumb and forefinger as instructed. Either this guy knew his business, or he'd seen lots of films. Dan worryingly suspected the former, as the man wouldn't come within ten feet of him – too far away to rush him, too close to move and have him miss with the first shots. He was carrying an automatic rifle and was dressed in camouflage clothing.

Dan slowly turned to face him. Everything about the man screamed professional soldier. Early forties he would guess, lean, not very big, but something behind the eyes made him believe this guy was figuring out whether to kill him now or later.

"Talk," he barked.

Dan decided that nothing other than full disclosure would get him out of this. "I'm from a group of survivors; we have women and children and they need protecting. I came here to try and find better weapons and hopefully more people to join us," Dan rattled off. "We need your help."

The man considered this for a time, and gestured with the muzzle of his rifle for Dan to walk. Dan went slowly and kept his hands up and away from the knife visible on his rucksack strap. He tried a few times to get the man to speak, but he was just ignored. Dan found himself back at his Land Rover, where he was ordered to produce the keys. He was sure he was going to be robbed, and faced a cold night with an uncertain journey back, but to his surprise he was told, "Wait here. I'll be back in an hour."

"What?" said Dan, and he looked back over his shoulder but the man was gone. Where he was standing were his rifle and pistol.

He considered the situation he was in, and decided that it was worth the risk to wait. If an ambush were planned, nobody would take the risk of arming their intended victim. It made no logical sense, so Dan stowed his gear, poured a lukewarm coffee, and lit a cigarette.

Just under an hour later, he heard an engine. He put himself on the other side of his Defender and waited. A roofless military version of his own car arrived towing a small covered box trailer painted in military colours with netting tied up on the sides. The man got out of his own vehicle, which was left running, quickly scanned a 360-degree sweep, and unhitched the trailer in silence.

He climbed back into his own Land Rover, looked at Dan, and said, "You'll not come back here again." It was a statement, not a question.

Dan hitched up the trailer and made his way down the road, not wanting to consider the consequences of attempting a refund or exchange.

THE SOLITARY SENTRY

For someone who had spent twenty years surrounded by fellow soldiers, the sergeant now felt so terribly alone. There were three squadrons based at the barracks, along with permanent support staff attached. Usually only one squadron was there at a time in full, the others either being deployed overseas or away somewhere training.

Some days there were very few people around, and permanent training staff like him could do as they pleased. It was one of those places that ran itself, and officers were lucky to be there, not like most camps where the officers dictated everything.

When it happened, there were fewer than thirty people on site. Many of the married soldiers had houses nearby, and only the singles really stayed in the base. Of the thirty, only he had survived. He didn't understand any of it. He went into the intelligence cell for answers and found only bodies. He armed himself and set a patrol routine as he waited for orders to come. He watched a few people pass by, never stopping or threatening his post.

He was a man of conscience; he would never allow the sanctity of his base to be breached by any outsider, and he would defend it with his life, but the man who came had said something that had affected him deep down.

He had women and children to protect.

The sergeant couldn't ignore that, but he couldn't abandon his post or invite outsiders in. He decided to offer what little assistance he could without breaking the rules too much. After he was alone again, he lapsed into the start of a depressive cycle that he could not escape.

He was a professional soldier, a trained killer, and he had seen active service on four continents and taken a fair toll on the enemies of Her Majesty.

None of that made a damned bit of difference anymore, because he was alone.

BIG BOY TOYS

Dan had set up for the night in a small roadside fuel station. He had to put on his gloves and mask to drag two bodies out of the back door, followed by three bin bags of rotting food. He wound up two of his camping lights and hung them on the open doors of his new trailer. If this was a payoff to keep him away from the camp, it certainly worked.

He saw four modified M4 carbines, multitudes of magazines and boxes of 5.56mm rounds. Two pump-action shotguns, one with a full-length stock and the other had a pistol grip, with three boxes of cartridges. These weren't the normal cartridges he'd scavenged for hunting; these were heavy-duty slugs. People killers.

There was also a belt-fed support weapon, an old general-purpose machine gun with three whole crates of heavy belted ammunition for it. Another crate contained six Sig Sauer 9mm handguns, spare clips, and boxes of ammo. A Peli case contained two sets of night-vision goggles. There was another box of attachments for the M4s and shotguns. Reflex red dot sights, 4x zoom wide optics, torch mounts, and even a couple of suppressors.

Dan could hardly believe it: He'd gone to scavenge what he could find and had been gifted enough weaponry to start a war. He had more guns than he had people to use them.

He put the hunting rifle in the back, along with the box of .22 rounds for it, and selected himself an M4: short-barrelled with a front vertical grip, full-length rail, and no carry handle. He took a mid-range combat scope, a box of magazines, and a box of ammo inside. As he moved the contents of the trailer around, he uncovered a dark tan vest. He pulled this out to find it was body armour, and had large and small magazine pouches and a pistol holster high on the front of the chest. The pouches were removable and could be put anywhere on the vest. A pipe was showing on the right shoulder strap, which turned out to be a water bladder.

He closed up the trailer and went inside. He found what he was looking for quickly, and returned with a heavy padlock, which he locked the trailer with.

He found a multi-tool thing that had Torx bits and Allen keys. With this, he fitted the scope, suppressor, and a right-side torch mount to his new toy. *Mental note: Find somewhere to sight the scope.*

He now carried four spare magazines for the M4 and one in the carbine. *Overkill*, he realised, but didn't really care. He loaded them all with fewer rounds than they would take at full capacity to minimise the risk of the weapon jamming. The spare clips for the Glock went on the vest too, after he unloaded and loaded them to ease the springs, and the pistol went into the chest holder. The leg holster wasn't that comfortable and kept catching on things, plus Neil always took the piss out of it and called him Lara Croft.

The M4 had a sling that he played around with, fixing it to the vest until he got it right. He could drop the weapon and it would hang vertically down from his chest and remove it by a clip if he wanted to. His smaller fixed blade knife went onto the left shoulder strap, and he considered fixing the machete to the back but decided not to. Definitely overkill.

He settled down on his makeshift bed after eating, happier.

He woke early, cold and slightly confused by a tapping noise. He rolled from the sleeping bag onto one knee and raised the M4 in search of the source. The few seconds of brain fog from waking cleared and he realised he was hearing a crow on the tin roof of the small forecourt.

He rubbed his face and went about his post-apocalyptic morning routine: Brush teeth, wash face, dream of a hot shower and a shave. He was starting to look homeless, as he hadn't shaved for a week.

Shaking himself out of his grogginess, he packed his gear and took all the batteries and other consumables into the Land Rover. He boiled some water from a bottle he emptied off the shelf into the pan on his camp stove and drank the rest as he looked around some more.

Medicines, spirits, cigarettes all went into the car. He poured the boiling water into his rinsed thermos, tipped in some expensive instant coffee, and packed it. He made himself a cup with the leftover water and took a sip. It was good, so he threw in the four tins of coffee he found on the shelf.

The rest of the gear was stowed, and Dan set off towards his temporary home. He was sure the stress levels of some of the group would lower drastically if he got back sooner than expected.

He wound along the country roads much slower, as he wasn't very confident towing, and saw a woman standing with a horse behind the hedge on a small farm.

He stopped and steadied himself. It was worrying how quickly he was getting used to being alone. He got out of the car, leaving the carbine in the cab but locking it with the remote fob.

As he approached the woman, she turned calmly towards him and casually picked up an over/under shotgun that was resting on the gatepost.

"Hi. I'm Dan," he said. She studied him with almost a sarcastic look, making him feel a little self-conscious about his action man outfit.

"Hello, Dan, I'm Sera," she replied. She had a slightly country twang to her accent, as though she had been raised somewhere else but had been naturalised into the countryside.

"What are you doing here, Sarah?" he asked.

"It's Sera. S-E-R-A. And I'm looking after these horses, which is plainly obvious if you cared to use your eyes."

She fixed him with a stare that almost dared him to question her. He guessed she was mid to late thirties. She had natural dark blonde hair tied back in a ponytail and horse riders' thighs, he realised guiltily and quickly looked away. He saw her vehicle parked inside the field by the small stable block. It was a Nissan Pathfinder, liveried with a liberal amount of mud and the details of a veterinary surgery.

"Are you a vet?" Dan blurted out.

"Yes," Sera replied. "What are you?"

He was almost tempted to introduce himself as First Ranger, but decided that he was in danger of too much scorn already. "I'm part of a group of survivors based a couple of hours away. I'm looking for people to join us," he added hopefully.

"Not me, thanks. I have things to do here," she replied briskly, but softened the blow with a lopsided smile and rested the shotgun against the fence again.

He tried to convince her. Pleaded with her. He told her of the idea to find a permanent place to live, to raise livestock.

"We need you, don't you see?" he said.

"Maybe. But I don't necessarily need you, do I?" she replied. "I'm sorry, the idea seems nice and everything, but I have plenty to do here."

That seemed to be the end of the negotiations as far as she was concerned. Dan reckoned that she was living there, and wondered what he could do to convince her to come back with him. He turned to her again, to try to reason some more to see if he could wear her down.

She sighed, conveying a great deal of annoyance, and picked up the shotgun for a second time. It was time to leave.

Dan got the hint and walked away backwards. "If you change your mind, come and find us." He asked if she knew where the town they set up camp in was, and gave directions to find them.

Sera seemed not to be listening, but she watched him off the property. He had no choice but to continue his journey alone.

THOSE KINDS OF PEOPLE

Penny was happy in a way. She had purpose, and she had people who needed organising. She felt that she had to maintain that semblance of normality, or the one crack in the cup would shatter the whole tea set. She worried that she wouldn't be able to keep the house of cards she was building in one piece, not without the support of the stronger people.

She knew she needed him, and hoped that he felt he needed her too. She just wasn't accustomed to playing second fiddle to anyone. She'd been a head teacher for almost a decade now; it was her life.

She was happy to have James and Kevin out looking for supplies. She was certainly glad of having the ever-smiling Neil and the more mysterious but slightly intimidating and often recalcitrant Daniel. She was overjoyed to have Leah; a life without children wasn't something she had ever considered possible, even though she had never had her own. She was even glad to have Andrew, as weak-willed and malleable as he was, because at least he was no threat to them and he didn't expect a free ride.

She was more concerned with some of their new arrivals, however.

Of the four, Jimmy and Kev had brought two back. They were lovely people, and she was glad to have them.

About two hours after Dan and the others had left, two others strolled up to the camp. They were drinking beer from cans, and she thought they were both already drunk, which at that time of the day, she thought was utterly common of them.

Commonness was an insult she deemed quite serious.

Their clothing seemed new, as though they had just smashed a window for it the day before. She could hardly judge them for that in her new clothes and boots, but when she did it, it seemed far less like theft than the feeling that oozed from these two.

She faced a conundrum: Turn away two survivors because she felt they were undesirable, or allow them to stay and see if they could be helpful to anyone other than themselves.

After all, who was she to decide a person's fate? The power of life and death was not hers to serve out, Penny felt. She was not so naïve to realise that turning survivors away from shelter and safety was tantamount to a death sentence.

The two undesirables were greeted without prejudice. Luckily, Neil was back in the camp at the time, having brought back two caravans and another Land Rover with Andrew. Their set-up and plan was explained to the people around them. They did not introduce themselves until asked.

The female was called Chloe and had her hair pulled back tight and stuck down. She had big hoop earrings and was dripping with freshly looted jewellery.

The male was called Callum. He stooped and wouldn't stand up straight. He couldn't keep still, for that matter; he was constantly shuffling his feet or fidgeting with his face. His eyes were always scanning everything too. He had the look of a thief, decided Penny, and then silently chided herself for being judgemental.

Penny asked politely about their qualifications and experience. Her judgemental feelings burned brightly when she found that neither had ever worked or been educated past the compulsory stages. She couldn't help it: She thought these two were bad news, both about twenty years old and utterly useless to the society of last month, let alone that of today.

They were allocated a caravan and invited to take some time to rest before they helped Andrew and the others load the supply lorry. They went into the store after a while and Penny thought that she might actually be wrong, and that they would help the group.

The couple brought back by Jimmy and Kev were her kind of people. They were in their late fifties; Cedric was retired and drove community ambulances part-time and his wife Maggie was a dinner lady. Both caravan enthusiasts, they had loaded up their own 4x4 and caravan and were gathering more supplies when Maggie literally bumped into Kev. There had been some initial screaming, but they came back to the camp and fitted in well.

Penny had busied herself with preparing food and looked up to see Andrew, Cedric, Leah, and Maggie struggling out of the shop with trolleys full of bottled water. She asked where Chloe and Callum were, and received timid shrugs all around. Clearly, something had happened and none of them wanted to say.

"Please tell me what happened," Penny asked gently.

None of them wanted to say, to rock the boat, until Maggie finally blurted out that they asked them to help and the two just swore at them. "They haven't lifted a finger," she complained.

Penny smiled and told the four that they should take a break.

She marched into the store and eventually found Chloe and Callum in the alcohol aisle. Both were drunk and eating crisps as they sprawled on the floor in a sea of discarded cans and packets.

She stood in the aisle with her hands on her hips, waiting patiently for them to notice her. She saw them glance in her direction and both laughed. She drew herself up and loudly cleared her throat. This drew more giggles from them, so she stalked towards them and asked loudly, "What do you two think you are doing?"

"What?" said Callum, his voice dripping with scorn and disrespect. "We do what we want, yeah? What you gonna do? Fuck off, yeah."

This made Chloe laugh and agree, "Step off, old lady."

Both had that fake "street" accent that Penny had heard the more unfortunate children in her school use. Defeated, ridiculed, and irate, she paced angrily out of the shop and considered calling Neil back to deal with them. Without James and Kevin, she doubted she could force them to do anything, so she decided to wait until that night when Daniel returned. Hopefully.

Callum had never worked. He had never done anything to benefit anyone but himself, and what he did do usually hurt someone else but he never saw that as his problem. He had spent his life since his mid-teens in and out of young offenders' institutes, and he saw prison as nothing but another "tour" where he met old friends.

He was a parasite, and Chloe was no better. They were thieves. Lazy people who believed that the world owed them everything, and if someone said no to them, then they threatened and intimidated them until they got their own way.

Their parasitic lifestyle was about to meet an abrupt end, and neither of them had the slightest inkling.

As dinner was ready, Dan blessedly drove up towing a small army trailer. Penny walked to intercept him, and Neil joined her, having been briefed efficiently by her on their now resident squatters. They hadn't seen Chloe or Callum since the incident, and assumed they were still inside.

Dan wasn't given time to explain what had happened with his trip, but the new equipment didn't go unnoticed. They quickly filled him in about their troublesome new additions, and Penny saw his face descend into anger.

"New rule: work together or get out. They're leaving, now." He turned to Neil and said, "No guns, I'll deal with this."

Dan unlocked the padlock on the trailer and threw in all his new equipment. He went to meet the impending confrontation carrying no weapons, but was armoured in a temper that neither Neil nor Penny had seen before. The temper was nothing new to him; he had learned to channel it, to focus it, to use it. He'd spent years dealing with scum like this, and now there were no disproportionate rules in place to protect them from him.

He stomped towards the shop, ignoring everyone on the way as his adrenaline-fuelled muscles tensed in anticipation. He rounded the entrance to see Andrew flat against the wall, white with fear, and a chav leaning up into his face.

"You," Dan growled. "Put him down. Now."

Every word from Dan dripped with threat. Callum was either very brave, drunk, or had no natural sense of self-preservation.

"Who the fuck do you think you is, yeah?" he droned. A carving knife was produced in Callum's left hand, and he tried his hardest to swagger in Dan's direction. Had Dan still been carrying firearms, the situation would have formed differently, but Dan wanted this idiot to think he had the advantage, that Dan was yet another person he could bully and intimidate as he had his whole life. Andrew ran from the shop in panic.

"Where's your slag?" Dan barked at Callum, stopping him in his tracks.

Rage contorted Callum's face at the insult. The anger destabilised him, made him reckless, as Dan knew it would.

"Chloe!" Callum shouted, causing her to appear from around the corner with an armful of cigarette packets. "This fool thinks he's a big man. He's going to apologise for calling you a slag before I cut him up."

"No, I'm not. She's a slag, and you're a little boy playing hard man. If you both leave now, I'll let you go," Dan said in a very matter-of-fact way.

He knew full well how this would play out, and he wanted it to be public. He wanted Callum to be shamed in front of the group, and he didn't want to miss the opportunity to reinforce a learning point.

Dan was calm whereas Callum was shaking with anger. He turned his back on the boy with the blade and walked outside, where Andrew's panicked flight had drawn a crowd. The whole group was there to watch, and as Dan looked along the line of scared and confused faces, Callum erupted from the shop, helpfully shouting in rage to tell Dan exactly where he was. Screams and shouts of alarm erupted from the group.

Dan stepped quickly to the side and kicked out at Callum's knee as he passed. He dropped the knife and rolled around the floor, shocked and in pain. Dan walked around him, kicking the knife back to his grasp. Callum caught his breath, picked up the knife again in his left hand, and lunged for him. Dan blocked the lunge, driving a forearm into Callum's chest, but Dan kept hold of him to stop him falling down. Dan pushed him away and told him again, "I gave you the chance to leave unhurt. What happens now is on your head."

Callum changed tactic and started to slash wildly at Dan, who retreated one pace at a time until Callum went to cut down at him from height. Dan stepped in, blocking his arm with both hands and seizing Callum's wrist painfully, forcing the hand to bend and stretching the ligaments tight. The pain and the loss of power in his grip made Callum drop the useless knife from his limp fingers.

Dan drove his left knee hard under Callum's diaphragm, taking his legs out from under him. Dan kept hold of the wrist and hand and stepped into Callum, spinning him over his back and slamming him to the floor. As Callum went down, Dan turned and went to his knees with him, folding Callum's left arm over his own arm and locking it off. He readjusted his position and leaned back, causing a crack to sound from Callum's joints almost as loud as his scream. Callum went pale and fainted from the pain.

Chloe was still in the doorway, open-mouthed at what she had witnessed. She seemed unsure what to do, and as Dan stood and brushed his hands off, he fixed her with a look.

"Take one of the cars from the car park and leave. Now."

She hesitated, looking between the writhing Callum and Dan.

"Believe me, I have a problem hitting a woman, but when it comes to the safety of these people, I will make an exception for you," he said coldly.

Chloe snapped out of her trance and ran over to Callum. He had come around and was crying. She helped him up and half dragged him over to the car park. Neil, ever reliable, threw her a set of keys to an old Peugeot they had found on an unfortunate member of former shop staff and the group watched as they left.

A stunned silence still reigned over the group, and Dan realised they were all looking at him. He saw a mixture of smiles and looks of relief and gratitude, but also some shock and fear too. He was still fired up and didn't think that now was the time for a speech, but he had to address the fears he saw before they grew into doubts about being part of the group.

"I'm sorry you had to see that," he lied, "but I will go to any lengths to protect you all from people like that." He gestured towards the fading sound of the Peugeot's engine. "It had to be done that way. If they knew we had guns, they would be back to take them. We can't afford to trust our safety and our future to people like that; they were nothing to society last week, and trust me, they are more of a drain now."

He walked away, hopeful that he hadn't gone too far in proving his point and removing a problem. He caught a look from Leah as he passed, and swore that she was hiding a grin.

Neil jogged and caught up with him, and he turned to see Penny walking briskly towards him. She had too much decorum to run. Neil was smiling, clearly impressed with the demonstration, but he could not be sure that Penny would be amused.

She stopped short of him, and straightened herself to imply formality. "You have my thanks for doing that. I agree that those people had no place here, but I must insist that you do not repeat such behaviour in front of Leah. She must not think that violence is the answer to problems."

Dan was inclined to agree with her, but his heart was still beating fast. He rounded on her and drew himself up similarly. "Make no mistake, Penny, there are times when violence is the *only* solution. Without people here willing to put themselves out, we will all be dead within the year." He softened, realising from her look that he had upset her. "I am sorry, genuinely. Not that I did it, but that some of the group would be scared by it. But don't you see it also proves what I am willing to do to people who will try and hurt us?"

Penny swallowed, unwilling to provoke an argument to make her point any more clearly. "Yes, I understand. Dinner is waiting, and I have Leah keeping an eye on it. Please tell us how your trip went."

Dan gestured for them to follow towards his new trailer. As he retrieved the key from his pocket, he told them the story of what happened at the camp.

"The soldier knew his business; if he wanted to kill me, I would never have known he was there. We need people like that, but he wouldn't entertain joining us. He gave me these and told me never to come back." He opened the trailer and shone his torch inside, resulting in a low whistle from Neil. Penny looked alarmed and her mouth hung open.

Dan retrieved his vest and carbine and locked the trailer again. He gave a spare key for the padlock to Neil and decided aloud on some more rules.

"Only selected people will carry firearms. We decide on who they are. As it is, I don't want anyone but us touching any of these, and all the other weapons stay in here. Penny, you have a shotgun for emergencies here. Neil, I want you to keep your Glock with you at all times and take whatever you want from here when you go out. Other than that, nobody has the experience to use one of these, which makes anyone carrying one without any training more of a danger to themselves and others."

Dan flashed back to a conversation he'd had with Jimmy the day they met, when he asked him about guns. Jimmy laughed, and said he'd be happier with a crowbar and a Kev.

Dan waited for a nod of agreement from both of them and walked away to his caravan. He heated some water on the stove and poured soap in a washing-up bowl. He stripped down and washed himself off, using the water to shave, as the stubble was itching. He decided he should probably just give up and grow a beard in the long term.

He dressed in fresh clothes, black combats, boots, and a black polo shirt. Feeling clean always made him feel more refreshed. Drinking a bottle of water, he came out to join the group, where Neil met him and introduced him to Cedric and Maggie. They had helpfully brought their own accommodation, and were towing it properly with a relatively new Discovery. It dawned on him that if this group had a sponsorship deal, it would definitely be with Land Rover.

Jimmy sidled up to him with a smirk on his face and two cups of coffee in his hands. Dan looked around, as it was rare to see Jimmy without Kev three paces behind him. He saw Kev playing with Leah, and Leah was helping him make something. The café area indoors would have been better for their purposes now, but the smell inside was unpleasant for any length of time. To settle down here would be a bad move, he thought, so he pushed that out of his head.

Jimmy asked outright, "Where'd you learn kung fu?" which disarmed the serious nature of the question.

Dan shrugged, not wanting to sound like a geek and explain the difference between different martial arts disciplines.

"Well, I'm just glad I never tried to do you with that crowbar when we met. Cheers." Jimmy raised his coffee cup to Dan's and left him in peace, realising that he wasn't going to get any more answers than he already hadn't.

Dinner was a quiet affair, with Penny calling order to the evening meeting as they tucked into their tinned peaches straight from the cans.

"I think we can all agree that today has been a little stressful." That raised a few chuckles, and Dan thought that the group had accepted what he had done as a part of their new world. "I'd like to formally welcome Cedric and Maggie to our fold." Nods and smiles all around. "I know this may sound a little official, and the temptation is to break from the bonds of normal life, but I think it very prudent to maintain as much order as we can. We are hoping to build a cooperative society, and not a dictatorship." She smiled in a self-effacing way to show that she meant it as a joke, but seriously at the same time. "I'd like to hear from everyone as to their progress and ideas if that's OK? James and Kevin, how are we faring on the *scavenging* side?" She invested the word with a bit of theatre, again to detract from the seriousness.

"All good, Penny," replied Jimmy. "Working our way through the places marked for emptying. More hands would mean quicker work. We could do with another lorry too, if anyone sees one."

"Very good," said Penny. "Everyone keep your eyes peeled for a large goods vehicle we can borrow. Neil," she said, moving on, "engineering?"

Never one to miss an opportunity to showcase, Neil stood and saluted lazily. In the languid style of a privileged young military officer educated at Eton, he said, "Yah, I've got a few hundred litres of diesel in jerrycans. More fuel cans are needed, but I'd prefer a trailer tanker. Nothing too big, you understand." A few laughs came from the captive audience for his perfect delivery of the character. Satisfied with having lightened the mood, he continued in his normal voice, sitting down, "Seriously, though, fuel isn't a problem right now. When we have more people and vehicles on the fleet, so to speak, I'll need to go further afield. We've got plenty of petrol to run the master keys too."

The master keys were what Neil referred to as the disc cutters – an accurate description when used in that capacity, Dan thought.

"Daniel?" Penny invited, unsure whether to mention his excursion.

Dan decided not to keep too many secrets from the group. "I've recovered weapons and ammunition to arm a few people well. My hope is to recruit more people with the necessary skills to do what I do, and to protect the group when I'm not here." Based on what they'd seen earlier, no arguments were raised. "If anyone has experience with weapons, I'll consider if they should have a gun."

Again, no arguments.

"OK," said Penny, "does anyone else have any ideas they would like to suggest?"

Cedric cleared his throat. "I'd like to suggest that I make a trip to some camping stores. I have an idea to set up some chemical toilets if that's OK?"

It was agreed that this was a good idea.

Dan thought that now was a good time to suggest the idea he had. "I've been thinking about a permanent site." That got everyone's attention, as he felt that they might be getting accustomed to life in a Morrisons car park. "There are prisons nearby that I think would be a viable option. There is a farm there which could sustain us long term if we had more people. I want to check it out tomorrow and I could do with an extra pair of hands to take notes for me." He looked at Leah and she beamed, looking to Penny and pleading for permission with her big eyes.

"Very well, young lady. Early bed for you then."

Leah skipped off, happy for the first time ever to be sent to bed early.

THE GRANGE

They rose early. Dan emerged to find the water boiling, rain falling gently, and Leah shuffling her feet with excitement.

"Morning," he said. "Have you got your bag packed?"

Leah dashed off and returned with a rucksack. She had bottles of water and snacks to last a few days, as well as a new notepad and pens. She was wearing her new walking boots and trousers, with her waterproof over a T-shirt.

"OK then, get some breakfast and do your teeth. We'll set off soon."

Dan walked over to see Cedric topping off his tank. Maggie was going with him, which didn't seem negotiable. Cedric planned to find a trailer and bring back the chemical toilets and associated things. Dan talked him through what to do if they encountered anyone: If they were friendly, then bring them back; if not, stay well clear. He gave them a local map and asked them to mark anything they thought was worth scavenging.

Neil was planning to stay local again, as agreed; the industrial estate was turning out to be a gold mine, and he was planning to find more vehicles for carrying what he found. He was getting ready to head out with Jimmy and Kev to get them a new lorry for their day's work.

Andrew was standing close to Penny, clearly struggling with having to do physical labour but lacking the temperament to argue or complain. Penny was listing off the things he should prioritise loading today. The list was shorter, as he was working alone.

Dan packed his bag after breakfast and filled his flask with coffee. As an afterthought, he wandered into the shop and grabbed two bags of sweets for the car. He noticed a car charger for an iPhone too and picked one up.

He donned his vest, checked his weapons, and got into the Land Rover. Leah was there in a flash and jumped in the passenger's side. He produced the sweets, and her eyes lit up – it hadn't dawned on her that she no longer had to wait for permission to have things now, and she was happy. He gave her the car charger for her phone and she was so excited that she struggled to open it. Dan had to use his knife to get through the packaging, and she plugged it in, desperately watching the screen for it to come to life.

As he drove off, he saw Penny. She mouthed *Be careful!* at him and he nodded in acknowledgement.

About two miles down the road, Leah's phone came to life, and she checked for messages. That hadn't dawned on her yet either.

"It won't work, chick. Just leave it plugged in so you can play games later, OK?"

She reluctantly put it down and paid attention to where they were going. They arrived in about ten minutes at the large pub Dan had painted. He saw that Leah looked at everything, but never seemed to nag with questions. He didn't know if she was like that before or not.

They drove into the turning for the prisons, and saw that the landscape opened up. A farm was visible at the top of the hill and looked very promising. Despite having lived on a farm as a child, he didn't know much about how one should be run. He really could have done with his dad right now.

He avoided going to the large prison, as he knew it would be sealed up tight without power. Instead, he drove down to the old manor house, converted to a prison years ago. This was the open prison, where the lower-risk people saw out the end of their sentences. He drove slowly down the picturesque driveway until he came to a barrier, and much to Leah's amusement, he drove straight through it, snapping it off.

The Grange itself was a lovely building. He knew it had beds for a couple of hundred people, kitchens, stores, and even a gym. Combine that with the farm and the workshop, and they could live comfortably with enough people to do all the necessary jobs. Now for the difficult part.

"Leah, I need you to wait in the car." She looked disappointed, like it was the end of the world all over again. "I mean it, doors locked, and you hang on the horn if you see anything. OK?"

"Fine," she said. "I've seen dead bodies already, you know," she added petulantly.

Dan decided a bit more honesty was in order. "Me too. I've seen lots, but I didn't see *any* until I was a few years older than you, and I've never seen – or smelled – two hundred of them in one building. End of." That got no further argument from her.

He got out and she locked the doors. He chambered a round in the M4 and applied the safety, then checked the chamber of the Glock and holstered it.

He walked up to the front door; there was no need for stealth because he didn't want to surprise anyone. He found it unlocked. He walked in and looked to his right where the security office was. Looking at the in/out ledger there, he saw no activity for nearly a week. He imagined that the virus, or whatever it was that wiped everyone out, would have spread very quickly in here. The whiteboard in the office gave a roll call of one hundred and eighty inmates, written directly above the body of a dead prison officer who was starting to smell.

He walked through the lower floor, going room to room, and found only another half a dozen bodies. He went back outside to check on Leah and found her playing on her phone. She took a while to notice him and looked guilty when she saw him staring at her from ten feet away.

"If you're with me, eyes open. Play later, understood?" She did. He told her he was going back in and to follow the same rules.

Heading upstairs, he cleared the other rooms, floor by floor. Some were locked, but a set of keys retrieved from the office downstairs let him through everywhere. The bonus was that nearly all the locks fit a certain pattern of key, so there were only really a few to choose from.

In total, Dan counted fewer than eighty bodies. He imagined that as soon as there wasn't enough staff to stop the flow, most who weren't already sick would have abandoned ship at the first opportunity.

This place will be perfect, he thought. It had everything they needed to sustain them. It just needed clearing, cleaning, and repopulating.

He jogged back outside to the Land Rover to find Leah doing her best impression of a meerkat.

He decided to check out the farm, and as he turned the car around in the ornate turning circle in front of the building, Leah asked what notes she should make.

"Perfect. Kitchens, bedrooms, storage, gym, farm. Needs clearing. Seventy plus. Petrol and a trailer."

Leah wrote it all down in neat handwriting, as best as she could in a moving car, and asked Dan to repeat it until she had it all down. He saw a concrete fenced area which looked like an unused tennis court about a quarter mile from the house.

"Tennis court for fire disposal," he said to Leah, nodding at her notebook.

The farm was perfect too. It had a few tractors and trailers, and other heavy equipment like a telescopic forklift as well. Not like the small factory ones, but a huge four-wheel-drive, rough-terrain one.

He heard pained bellowing from one of the sheds, and saw that a dozen cows were shut in. He looked around and found that the nearest field was empty. He asked Leah if she was OK with animals, and she shrugged, eager to get out of the car. They opened the gates and let the cows into the field. They would be useful in the future, but not if they starved to death in the sheds. The water troughs were full, topped up with the rain, and the cows eagerly pushed in to get a drink. He did the same with the penned pigs – those that still lived – and put them in a muddy pen outside. He found feed and scattered it for the pigs; the cows were happy with the plentiful grass.

A large chicken shed with outside runs held plenty of birds too. He placed empty buckets in all of the outside pens to collect rainwater. A few chickens had died, and Dan collected them up and threw them into the pigpen. Best not explain that one to Leah. He did the same with all the eggs too.

It was better than he had hoped for again. He just needed people who knew how to run a small farm. They drove back to the main prison building and took the route behind the manor house. There were sports fields behind, another outbuilding which looked like a classroom, and the remains of the previous manor that looked to have subsided long before he was born. The gym was a separate building set by the large woodland and was well equipped, as he expected a prison gym to be. He asked Leah to note that two needed recovering from there.

"Two dead bodies in the gym, got it," she said, writing. So much for shielding her from all this, then.

They followed a dirt track past the gym that led to a very large lake. Dan didn't have a fishing permit like the signs stated were mandatory, but he also doubted that anyone around cared any more.

They sat by the lake, which also had an abundance of Canada geese, and ate their snacks. He moved to sit on the bonnet of the Land Rover and lit a smoke to complement his coffee.

"What do you think then, kid?" he asked Leah.

She opened her notebook and said, "Perfect location. Bedrooms, kitchens, storage and a gym. About seventy bodies to carry to the tennis court to be burned. Farm has cows, chickens, and pigs. Gym needs clearing and the lake has fish and geese." She smiled at Dan, eager for praise.

"Excellent," he said, "but do you like it?"

"It'll do," she said with a smile.

RECRUITMENT DRIVE

After an hour walking around the manor grounds and checking all the smaller buildings, they returned to the Land Rover just as Leah was starting to flag a little. She got in and started on the sweets.

They decided to recce a bit further afield and drove on towards the next town where Dan had found Kev and Jimmy. They went slow, and twice Leah scared the life out of him by shouting when she saw something. So far, they had seen a couple of vehicles they wanted – another lorry with a tail lift, and a transit tipper. Dan wanted that for loading dead bodies into and emptying the rotting cargo onto the tennis court where he planned to burn them, but again he thought it best to leave out the details for Leah. The tipper was in a small commercial van lot, which was marked on the map as a priority.

As he was looking through the windows of the small portacabin office, he heard the Defender's horn sound once. He sprinted back, carbine raised and switched to semi-automatic. He saw Leah pointing frantically ahead of her at two people in the distance. They seemed frozen still, and Dan raised the M4 to see them through the 4x optic.

A man and a woman were squinting towards him, trying to figure out the sound they had heard. The girl obviously had the better eyesight, as she made out Dan pointing a gun at them first. She turned and fled, the man confused but following her regardless.

He swore to himself. *Mental note: find some small binoculars.* He started the Land Rover and sped off in the direction they had run. Leah was bombarding him with questions, all of which he ignored as he scanned around him for signs of where they went. He reached a T-junction at the end of the road. A choice he'd been faced with many times over his years of chasing people was ahead.

"Left or right? Left or right?" he repeated. Better to make a choice and have a fifty/fifty chance of being right than hesitate too long and guarantee failure.

"Left," said Leah, pointing helpfully left.

"Can you see them?" Dan asked.

"Downhill," she said. "You don't run away uphill," she said, explaining basic logic to an experienced hunter of people.

He didn't have time to be impressed, which he was, but tore off left, accelerating hard and kicking himself for missing the obvious. Target focus: schoolboy error. He saw a flash of movement on the left side, just as Leah called out, "There!!"

The girl had sharp eyes. The two had indeed run downhill, and when they had heard the car coming after them, they had decided to jump a garden wall and try to hide.

Dan skidded the Land Rover to a stop and went to get out. Leah stopped him by flapping her right arm at him.

"Don't scare them. Let me talk," she said with a maturity that surprised him.

"What?" he asked.

"You're moody and you look a bit scary," she replied with devastating honesty.

"Fine," he said, "just wind the window down though."

Leah held down the electric window button.

"Hi," she tried. It was almost funny, as an obvious pair of shoes were visible sticking out from behind the bins.

"We are nice! Honestly," she called out again. "We want people to come and join our camp. I'm only twelve and they look after me. I know he looks scary; he scared me when I first saw him, but he's the one who protects us."

Dan held his breath for a while, until his patience snapped and he went to get out. He stopped, seeing the two emerge from their hiding place.

The girl came first, tentatively followed by the male. They both looked mid-twenties and terrified. Leah reassured her, telling her it was OK.

"Please," the girl said, "my friend, he have accident. Very bad." Her English was heavily accented and sounded Eastern European. She had dark hair in thick curls and a slightly olive-skinned complexion. The male behind stepped forward; he looked very nervous.

"It's true," he blurted out fast, "our mate got hit on the head by a crate that fell off the shelves." He sounded like a local. He looked thin, a bit scruffy with off-the-poster tattoos on both forearms. "We were going to the pharmacy to get bandages and stuff."

"Where?" asked Dan.

"The shop, down from here," said the girl, pointing back towards where he had first seen them.

"Not the pharmacy. Where is your mate?" He knew where the pharmacy was; he had emptied it the other day with Jimmy and Kev.

"We can show you," said the male.

Dan gave this careful consideration, as he had Leah with him. He couldn't ask her to keep a gun on them, nor could he cover them and drive. He had to choose whether to trust them or not.

"Get in," he said. "Throw those bags into the back."

As they climbed in, he unfastened the Velcro strap of the holster on his vest for easier access should he need the gun.

Leah smiled at him, completely unaware of the risk he had just taken for them both.

"I am Ana," said the girl. "This Kyle," she said, pointing to the man. Her accent made her pronounce Kyle as Keel.

"Dan. Leah," he said, gesturing to them in turn. "Where is your friend?"

They drove for a few minutes, taking lefts and rights on Ana's direction. They arrived at a small Sainsbury's store, not a supermarket but a smaller shop. Dan spent as much time watching them in the rear-view mirror as he did looking forwards.

"There's five of us," said Kyle, who seemed either wary or in awe of Dan. "John tried to get something down from the stockroom this morning. We found him out cold after we heard the crash."

Dan stopped the car and the two new passengers got out. He didn't know whether to make Leah wait in the car again, but decided he wanted her in his sight instead.

They followed Ana and Kyle through the shop to an office where John was laid out on the floor covered with a blanket. He was breathing in short, shallow snores. Two other people, another man and woman, were kneeling at either side of him.

"What happened? How long has he been like this?" Dan asked as he walked in. The two unknowns looked shocked to see a heavily armed man burst in and bark questions. He took one look at the head wound on John and turned to Leah, handing her the Land Rover keys.

"My bag in the boot. Open the top, take out the separate bag. Go now." She ran off, taking the keys. Dan looked to Ana, who silently followed her.

Kyle answered the questions.

"A box of tins fell and hit him in the head. He's been like that for about five hours." It seemed like they had just dragged him into the office where he now lay and were waiting for him to wake up.

Dan clipped the torch off the front mount of the carbine and slung the gun round on his back. He called John's name loudly in his face and got no response. He opened his right eye, then his left, shining the torch in both before moving it away and repeating.

Bad news. John's pupils were unevenly dilated, and neither responded to the bright LED light shone into them. He had seen this before, head injuries where people seemed dead drunk or totally sound asleep but they were never going to wake again. He felt down John's upper body, and stopped when he felt crunching in John's spine at the bottom of his neck.

Dan was no consultant, but he was experienced enough to know that John had a possible broken neck, and was likely brain-dead from the impact. He had no idea how to deliver this news to three people he didn't know, so he busied himself by continuing to check him over. Even a month ago, with CT scans and neurosurgeons, he doubted whether John would have survived this accident. John had wet himself at some point; the smell of dried urine burned Dan's throat.

Leah burst back in carrying Dan's trauma kit, and he took it and applied a fresh dressing to John's head to cover some time.

"OK, let's give him some air," he said with authority. He always found that with people who had little or no first aid knowledge, if you gave them firm commands, they did as they were told.

The six of them who were still alive stepped out into the shop. Dan opened a can of coke from the now useless chiller and drank deeply.

"I'm Dan, and this is Leah. We're from a group a little way away, and we're looking for other survivors. We've met Ana and Kyle…" He trailed off, looking at the other two who hadn't been introduced.

The female seemed to wake up first. "I'm Lexi," she said.

Everyone looked at the male, who eventually said, "Ian."

Silence hung over them for a few seconds. Dan didn't know how to tell them that John was effectively dead and would never wake up. Ana started with their story, how she had been wandering around until she met Ian and John. Kyle turned up the day after, and Lexi only last night. Dan tried to steer the conversation towards their previous lives, feeling a little mercenary, as he was trying to find out how useful they were to the group.

Ana had emigrated from Romania last year. She spoke Russian and English, and worked in a factory. She loved being in the UK, up until nearly a week ago. Leah was quick to interrupt and ask why she didn't speak Romanian, but learned that where she came from they spoke Russian.

Kyle worked in a supermarket and Lexi was a retail manager.

Ian was a lorry driver – finally, someone useful – but he seemed almost catatonic.

Most annoyingly, John owned a central heating and electrical company. *Just my luck*, thought Dan.

He finished his coke and packed up his trauma kit.

"Pop that away for me, please?" he asked Leah nicely. She skipped off and Dan straightened to address the four strangers.

"Bad news, I'm afraid. John has a broken neck and the head injury has caused permanent damage." He got nothing but blank looks in return. "John has no brain function. Even if we had a brain surgeon and a fully working hospital, he is still effectively dead."

They seemed to take it well. Nobody seemed affected at all, but then again, none of them had known him for more than a few days.

Dan continued, "I want you all to come with us. There are seven of us, maybe more by the time we get back, and we have good supplies. What's more, we have a permanent site lined up."

Leah walked back in before any of them could answer. She sensed that grown-up talk had just happened while she was out, and she looked at Dan waiting to be brought up to speed. When no immediate answer came, she asked, "How many are coming with us, then?"

He liked Leah's ice-breaking techniques.

"I'm in," said Kyle.

"I want come with you," Ana said to Leah, smiling.

"Yes," said Lexi.

Dan looked at Ian, who still seemed in shock. "Ian, we really could do with someone who can drive the heavy stuff. You coming?"

Ian slowly looked up at Dan, and then glanced to where John was.

"Yeah," he croaked, "but what about John?"

They all filled their bags with whatever they could. Dan had to put one of the boot seats down to have enough space to drive the six of them back. He was the last out of the shop, and thanks to the suppressor, nobody had heard the single shot that gave John peace.

Some truths were easy to ignore nowadays.

HOUSE MOVING

Their contingent of six got back to camp in the late afternoon. Lexi was the most alert and capable of them, so she drove the tipper van after Dan had opened the door and got the keys. Introductions were made to Penny and Andrew. Then Neil and his new recruit, when he rolled back in minus the fanfare he was hoping for. He was towing a small tanker trailer – a thousand litres, he bragged – behind another off-road-prepared Defender. Both were found tucked away on the industrial estate, and he was emphatic about their newly acquired fuel-storing capability.

Cedric and Maggie had returned, and not only had they set up the toilets, but they had also cleared out the covered trolley bay and erected a series of individual tents too. Cedric had left the trailer he had used to carry the equipment by the covered area. Hopefully Dan thought this was in preparation for moving.

Amazingly, their numbers had almost doubled in a day; Dan and Leah had brought back Ana, Kyle, Ian, and Lexi.

Cedric and Maggie had found a teenage boy and a woman in her thirties. Liam was seen walking along the road, and Kate drove up to them in the most unlikely of vehicles. Liam seemed only to mourn the loss of his Xbox, but Kate was a find of pure platinum. The group now had a paramedic in their own well-equipped ambulance. She was fit – a runner, Dan reckoned – and shared his sense of rebuilding society. Dan made a point of taking her aside and asking for a second opinion on John's symptoms, just in case he had been wrong. Luckily, she agreed, and he gave her the heads-up that she may be asked the same question after what he had done.

She had a very pragmatic sense of duty, and now that the law didn't apply, her views on euthanasia were no longer unpopular or deemed too liberal. She was tattooed, pierced, and, Dan strongly suspected, a lesbian. Nothing seemed to shock her, which he could only see as a plus point.

Neil had found himself a friend, a lad in his late teens who called himself Jay. Jay's dad had owned a landscape gardening business and he had seen his fair share of trees felled.

Dan's mental notepad was being scribbled on furiously.

Jimmy and Kev returned about an hour later in a new lorry. Sandwiched in the middle seat between them was another young man, Adam.

Adam was in the bathroom-fitting business. The family business as was, and he seemed a fit and healthy addition.

Penny had prepared another large meal of something Dan barely recognised as macaroni and cheese. Everyone ate and sat talking. An air of actual happiness had overtaken them with the new arrivals. After dinner, Penny called for some hush.

"Welcome to our new members. We are so thoroughly grateful to have you here." Noises of agreement came from the group. "I never thought I'd say this, but we are suddenly short on living space!" A few laughs from the circle. "James and Kevin, as agreed, you two will move into shared accommodation with Daniel and Neil."

Kev looked at Jimmy and raised his eyebrows.

Jimmy quietly said to him, "We're sleeping in their caravan." Kev smiled and nodded, leaning around to smile at Dan.

"Liam, Jay, you two will take James and Kevin's former caravan with Adam and Kyle." All those mentioned by name looked around and nodded. "Andrew, if you could please welcome Ian?" Nods of agreement were exchanged. "Leah and I will accommodate Lexi and Ana."

With sleeping arrangements sorted, Penny carried on. "Now, normal business will be suspended tomorrow morning until we have met to discuss our plans, so everyone must feel free to have a small drink and have a slightly later night. I say we have all earned it to get this far." She stood, and Dan thought she might have had a couple of those sherries while cooking.

"We have all of us lost a great deal," Penny continued. "Let us not think of loss, but consider our gains. We have all gained a new family in each other. May that family grow and prosper. Cheers!"

They drank. Leah was asleep in the chair before long, and Dan carried her into her caravan. He loaded and unloaded the magazines for his guns, ran a scrap of oiled cleaning cloth tied to the end of a piece of wire through the M4, and locked the carbine away before joining Neil in another journey to the bottom of a bottle.

He woke early, in desperate need to pee. Despite their new toilet setup, he went to the side of the building as before and pissed noisily against the wall. He decided that Neil was a bad influence, which would probably ruin his liver. He was never much of a drinker before; he would drink after rugby matches and always had drinks in at home, but he was never that much of a social drinker. He'd stopped going out to get drunk over fifteen years ago. Maybe the apocalypse was making him alcoholic.

"Who gives a fuck?" he croaked in answer to his own unasked question.

Others were starting to surface, and he saw Penny boiling a kettle and holding her head in obvious discomfort. He knew that look, and he knew that a strong cup of tea would do nothing for it.

When they eventually gathered, all with the exception of Leah, and sat around eating breakfast bars and drinking hot drinks, Dan decided to rouse his new assistant to help with the presentation. He banged on the door of the caravan and called her. "Leah, I need you and your notebook out here."

She surprised him by appearing within ten seconds. She was wearing pyjamas, had her hair mussed over her face, and stomped off to the toilets in her unlaced walking boots. She returned and sat down with a carton of fruit juice, producing her notebook. "Continue," she said to him sarcastically.

"OK, everyone, listen up. As some of you know, Leah and I went to check out a permanent site yesterday. Leah, what did we learn?"

Leah cleared her throat and said, "A prison. A big posh house prison and not like the telly. It has lots of bedrooms and offices and storerooms and a kitchen. There's a gym and a lake with fish and geese. There's a farm too, and we let the cows and the pigs and the chickens out."

Nobody spoke, but some hangovers were shaken a little clearer by the succinct intelligence report coming from the youngest person there.

"There are around eighty bodies to be cleared. Dan thinks we need a trailer and some petrol. The tennis court is the best –"

"Long story short," said Dan to cut her off, acutely aware of the cold, furious stare he was receiving from Penny, "the location is –"

"Perfect," interrupted Leah. Dan looked hard at her without speaking. "Continue," she said again, with a lavish gesture to him.

Cheeky cow, he thought. "Anyway, yes. It's perfect. However, it needs a couple of days' work to clear it and clean it. We have all the materials we need for that right here, but I think this should be our top priority as of now."

Nobody raised an objection, so he pressed on, taking the silence for consent. "All the food in there that is going off, and all the stuff in the bags over there," he said, gesturing to the store and to the pile of black bags removed over the last few days, "need to be taken to the farm, where it is feed for the pigs and chickens. We also need as many strong hands, and strong stomachs, as can manage the clearance of the building. The quicker we do this, the quicker we live under a roof again. Any objections?"

There were none. Dan almost forgot that Penny had declared an unofficial bank holiday and was about to set people off to work until he remembered. "We start the day after tomorrow, then!"

NOBODY EXPECTS THE INQUISITION

That afternoon, when people had slept a little longer, washed, and rehydrated, Penny began to call the new arrivals in for a deeper background check.

She invited Dan, Neil, and Jimmy to accompany her, and Dan was surprised to see Kate on the interview panel with them. Penny seemed to have selected a Head of Medical Services.

She started explaining the rules of the group, and asked each new person to account for their actions since the "incident."

Ninety-nine per cent of life was wiped out, and Penny still refused to use emotive language.

The questioning went on, and covered employment history, qualifications, vocational experience, and strangely, a new category had appeared in the interviews: "What would you like to be in the new society?"

Kate was exempt from this, unless, as Dan suspected, it had already been done privately. As the respective heads of department (Medical, Base Camp, Operations, and Engineering), they spoke to each person in turn until everyone in camp knew what was going on. A small queue formed as they were speaking to the first person: Kyle.

Kyle had GCSEs. He worked a checkout. He couldn't drive. He had no injuries or illnesses. Kyle wanted to be a Ranger and have a gun, but he offered no previous experience to support this and was assigned to assist Jimmy's scavenging teams. He was unhappy with it, but he didn't argue.

Ana had no formal qualifications. She worked on a factory line. She could not drive. She was fit and well. She raised livestock with her family before coming to the UK. Ana was temporarily assigned to the base camp, with a view to her tending their new livestock very soon. The rules of this were simple: Keep the animals alive.

Lexi was a deputy manager at Primark. She had a Higher National Diploma in Business Studies. She could drive. She was healthy. She had kept fit by learning jujitsu every week, and had even competed a few times. She was a former Army Cadet with experience with firearms and went running regularly. Dan agreed to assess her firearms skills, so Lexi was assigned to Ops as a potential Ranger as per her wishes.

Ian had come round significantly from yesterday. He could drive pretty much anything on wheels. He also knew a lot about solar panels, as he worked for a company that distributed them.

"It's amazing how much you pick up about stuff when you're waiting three hours to unload it," he joked.

Neil snapped Ian up straight away: A lorry driver who could get them hot water and electricity from solar panels in the long run? He was assigned to engineering, effective immediately.

Adam was a tiler and knew a lot about plumbing too. He drove a large van most days. He was a bit of a fitness fanatic. Jimmy took him as driver for a second scavenging team with Kyle, and promised him training on using the master keys.

Jay was taken by Penny to be "man about the house." He was qualified to use a chainsaw, and Dan thought that he was either going to end up as an enormous lumberjack, or he would have to find a log-splitting machine with all the wood he would have to chop.

Liam was a sullen youth, constantly moaning about the lack of electricity. The fact was, they had generators and could power televisions and the like. Nobody seemed to want to, though, and there seemed no point in using up a limited resource just to keep Liam happy. He was hard work. He was nearing his GCSE exams and would never actually finish high school now.

Liam wanted to be anything that had a gun, so Dan objected to him on principle.

"It's a burden. A heavy one, not a toy," Dan warned, but he could tell he was trying to lecture someone who had grown up playing *Call of Duty* and probably thought he could shoot. *Takes more than your thumbs, kid,* Dan thought.

Liam was allocated to be under Andrew's – the newly appointed Head of Supplies – care. Liam would have to learn to take stock inventory.

When they had finished, Penny recapped and produced her notes to the others:

Operations

Dan – First Ranger

Ranger (proposed: requires assessment and training) – Lexi

Engineering

Neil (Head)

Ian

Cedric – vehicle and fuel recovery

Logistics

James (Head) and Kevin – team 1

Adam and Kyle – team 2

Agriculture/Horticulture

Ana – livestock maintenance

Maggie – vegetable grower

Medical

Kate (Head)

Catering

NEED A COOK! (Penny in the interim)

Leah - helping

Jay - general

Supplies/Inventory

Andrew (Head), Liam as apprentice.

The new heads of department looked over her notes. Dan noticed she had put herself in as the temporary cook; however, it was very clear that she was the head of the group in most ways. They discussed whether they should wait where they were for a few more days or start clearing the prison as soon as possible. Dan pointed out that the sooner they moved the bodies, the easier and better. Kate seconded him; as a paramedic, she would have seen the results of bodies in various states of decay.

Dan claimed ownership of Ops, Engineering, and Logistics to clear the buildings. Penny agreed to follow with the caravans and supplies and everyone else to set up their new home the next day; she just wanted more time to load supplies. The only objection to this was that Kate offered to help with the clearance. Nobody argued against that. They parted, agreeing to take the rest of the day off and tell everyone that evening.

MAD MAX

That afternoon, Dan took Lexi out a few miles away to discuss her training and sight their guns. She had fired a handgun once, and had plenty of experience at shooting rifles on ranges. He ran through the basics of the role of a Ranger. He was making it up as he went along, trying to remember it for the next time. He broke down and built up an M4 in front of her, equipping it with the same 4x zoom optic as he used. He gave her the rifle, like his own weapon but with a slightly longer barrel with no vertical foregrip or suppressor, as she seemed more comfortable with it.

The Sig was a harder weapon to handle than the Glock, so he instructed her with his own gun; it was easier to use with smaller hands. They went into the industrial estate and he set up targets at ten and twenty feet. She was about 60 per cent accurate at twenty feet, which was good enough for him. He took the opportunity to sight his own M4 as she did hers. She remembered how, despite the years since she had held a firearm. Adjustments were made, and Dan saw she was eight for ten at what he guessed was a 150-metre range. Pretty damn good.

He kitted her out with one of the body armour vests, having to tighten it up as far as it would go, as Lexi had narrow shoulders and a fairly flat chest. He gave her the Glock and the spare magazines, and showed her how to load and unload them to ease the springs.

He ran through primary weapon failures and having to go to the secondary and reloading. He gave her a rucksack and a list of what she should take every time she went out, finally adding a couple of knives to her kit.

As he went over the rules for different scenarios with her at the armoury trailer, he stripped, oiled, and rebuilt a Sig to replace the gun he had given to Lexi. He loaded three magazines, set two of them neatly in place on his vest, and slapped the third one home in the gun. He racked the topslide to chamber a round. Looking at Lexi, he thought he should probably loot some black clothing for her too so that they didn't look too different. Uniforms, no matter how bizarre the situation, had a psychological effect on people.

As he was running through map skills and what kinds of buildings and vehicles to mark, she held up a finger to shush him and looked sharply to her left. Dan heard it at the same time and snapped into action. Unmistakably a motorbike, and what sounded like a person shouting and screaming like they were drunk or deranged. Dan decided to leave the Land Rover where it was, and they both approached on foot as fast as they could. Between them, they had nearly three hundred rounds of 5.56 ready to fire on full auto, and that was before they even used their pistols. Whatever it was they were hearing was unlikely to be a threat to them. He hoped.

As they neared the sound, they could hear a voice pleading for help. The word *no* was being screamed through sobs of pain, mostly drowned out by the motorbike.

Dan held his hand up and they both stopped. He saw a fixed steel ladder running up the side of a building with a flat roof, and pointed it out to Lexi. She nodded, slung her rifle, and ran to climb it. He knew she had a more than average chance of hitting anything she saw within a short distance and felt more secure having some top cover. When she reached the flat roof, Dan readied his carbine and rounded the corner at a crouch, knees bent and walking fast.

What he saw horrified him. A young man was riding a dirt bike around an older man. The older man was covered in cuts, and the rider was enjoying himself riding past the older man and making slices through his clothes with a machete not unlike Dan's. This kind of Mad Max shit made Dan very angry; people like that had such an ignorant understanding of anarchy – they thought it was a free ticket to rape. To maim those weaker. To prey on others.

The older man was trying desperately to protect a younger female by shielding her with his body. Dan would see no more of this man's blood spilled, so he flicked the safety catch to auto and fired three short bursts at the motorcyclist. *Fuck the verbal warning*, he thought with a savage flash of remembered anger; that was for a world with barristers who called you a murderer for doing your job.

The initial burst blew dust from the gravel in front of the bike. The second strafed up the front wheel and onto the instruments, and the last caught the man with three or four rounds from thigh to neck. The bike toppled instantly and stalled. By the time Dan reached the scene, still watching his target through optic and moving forward in a semi-crouch, the biker had died. Dan was just in time to see the last few weak spurts of arterial blood pulse from the ragged hole the bullet had torn in his neck.

Dan safetied and slung his M4 and bent down to the body. It looked like a fairly normal young man, not some crazed biker psychopath. Dan always believed that some people were just born bad, and this was one of them, just waiting for a situation to arise where he could throw off the bonds of acceptability, remove his mask of a normal person, and hurt other people for fun. Dan despised him, and felt no remorse for having ended his life without warning.

A scream from behind him made him spin around and drop to one knee. The hysterical girl who was being protected by the now unconscious and bleeding man had seen another would-be rapist enter the yard on another motorbike. Dan was thirty feet away, probably too far to be effective with the Sig, which he had never fired before, but he held the man in his sights and shouted a warning.

"Fucking leave, *now*. Do it now and I won't kill you," he shouted. The girl still screamed and keened in terror. The man he was aiming at looked past him at his dead comrade and revved his bike. Dan settled himself to squeeze off rounds systematically and try to bring him down. As Dan started to breathe out and squeeze, he saw the man shudder and fold over the handlebars, both body and bike hitting the ground together. A split second after the impact, he heard a sharp crack and the report of Lexi's rifle. Dan ran over, covering the body with his Sig, but found that the 5.56 bullet had shattered the guy's sternum and the heart behind it before blowing a small chunk of flesh out by the right kidney. Sick as it seemed, Dan was very happy with his new recruit's accuracy and timing.

He shouted at Lexi and asked if she was OK. She called that she was fine, and he told her to stay where she was and take out anything that didn't look friendly.

Dan sprinted back to the Land Rover and drove it back as fast as he could without losing his trailer. He knew he should administer emergency care where he was, but he needed to be out of the area and back to Kate sometime yesterday. Dan dragged the man and girl to the truck and forced them in; the man was barely conscious and bleeding badly, and she was in hysterics.

Dan jumped onto the bonnet, then the roof rack, and called Lexi to come down. She shinned down the ladder quickly by holding the sides and sliding, and then trotted around the side of the building to them.

"Three more bikes, a mile or so out, I think," she said.

He decided not to wait to be introduced – not that these two would ever speak again – and gunned the diesel engine hard back to camp.

HOW TO MAKE FRIENDS

Lexi had her head on a swivel on the way back as Dan concentrated on the driving. She checked the mirrors and kept turning to look behind in between shouting questions at the girl. "Who were those men? How many of them are there?"

The girl was incoherent, other than to cry "Dad" repeatedly at the unconscious man bleeding beside her. Dan caught a glimpse of his face in the mirror. He did not look good and was probably going into shock; the quicker he got the man to Kate, the better. They lacked the equipment to save him here; he needed more intravenous fluids than the one-litre bag Dan had scavenged so far.

They turned in hard to the camp and Dan sounded the horn three times before coming to a stop by Kate's ambulance. He was out of the Land Rover as it stopped, roaring her name. She appeared from Penny's caravan and her face suddenly dropped; she threw down her cup of whatever and ran towards them as Dan was dragging the unconscious man from the car. The girl was left there for now: Her immediate issues were mental, not time-critical or physical, and nothing could be done for her yet. Her dad was the one who needed treatment quickly. Kate shouted at Dan to put him on the bed as she started ripping open sealed packs and cutting his clothes off. Dan was the only other person in the group with medical knowledge, so he stayed and did as he was told, only pausing to unclip his M4 and rest it against the stretcher at the back. He told Lexi to get Neil and Penny, now.

They arrived as he was helping strip the unconscious man. "Lexi, Neil, get guns out of the trailer now. There's a group of hostiles about a mile south; we killed two and there were more. Lexi, top cover. Get up somewhere, on one of the lorries if you can, but get me eyes on now. Neil, load the tactical shotguns too. Go. NOW," he yelled as they were both standing, waiting for more orders.

Penny called to him, "What should I do?"

"Get everyone to load up. Use the last of the daylight to be ready to move ASAFP. We are moving tonight. DO IT!" he yelled, while helping Kate dress the least serious of the wounds – the ones that didn't require stitches to stop the bleeding. Kate was trying to find a vein to get fluids into the man, but had to resort to his neck, as he was already in shock due to blood loss. It looked likely that he would die.

Kate worked feverishly on the man.

"Kate, we need to move," Dan pressed her. She ignored him and continued to work.

He went outside the ambulance to see how the rest were doing breaking camp. The caravans had been hastily hitched and the 7.5-tonne trucks were started. It was a mess; people were split up just to get enough drivers behind wheels. Dan went to check on the girl and found her in a daze still in his Land Rover.

He saw people throwing bags into any vehicle they saw, and Neil had hitched his precious fuel tanker before throwing tools into the back of his own 4x4.

Lexi made eye contact with him and froze briefly before carrying on. He knew he would have to deal with the trauma forming in her head soon, but now wasn't the time. She had just killed someone without the time to reason why. That would hit her hard when the panic stopped.

Dan jumped back in the ambulance.

"Kate, either we move or we could all die," he told her.

"OK, that'll have to do," she said.

He closed the doors and did a last check of everyone. All were accounted for and their supplies were ready to drive, more or less.

"Sidelights only, follow me and be careful," he shouted, climbing behind the wheel.

FLY, THE ENEMY IS UPON US

He drove out of the car park, leaving behind months of food and fuel.

He didn't want to have to try and protect these people with his back to a wall; it was better to run.

He knew this was risky; he was asking untrained people under extreme stress almost blind with fear to drive unfamiliar large vehicles into the dusk, not knowing where they were going.

Better to set a slower pace than risk a pile-up.

His convoy crept north, keeping to the smaller roads to avoid pursuit. *Mental note: don't leave any more messages about our location until we are stronger.*

They wound through cars in the road, once having to use the Land Rover to push a crashed estate car out of the way to make room for the lorries.

After what seemed like an hour of checking the mirrors, expecting to see headlights hunting them down, they came to the prison. There was a large hardstanding at the front of the big house, and Dan halted the convoy there. He got out and waved the lorries past him and pointed them to a side area. The cars pulling caravans closed up, and he realised they'd had to leave one behind, as there weren't enough tow bars; it was better to prioritise the fuel over a temporary living space.

He called everyone in and took a knee, resting the butt of his carbine on the floor. "Well done, everyone," he said, looking around at the faces. He realised Kate was missing, probably tending to the man strapped to her stretcher. "Lexi, Neil, and I will keep watch tonight," he said. "Everyone, sleep with your boots on. If you hear shooting, then run to the back of this building and hide in the woods by the lake." He covered his thinking time by a tactical reload of his weapon, slapping in a full magazine in place of the one he had nearly emptied into Mad Max. He realised that people were looking at him in horror; he was covered in the man's blood.

"Try and get some rest, and we'll reassess in the morning." They took that as dismissal, and most faded away apart from Penny, Neil, Lexi, and Jimmy.

He saw Leah leading a shaking Kev by the hand. Maggie had climbed into the back of Dan's Land Rover to comfort the girl he had completely forgotten about on the drive here. She hadn't made a sound.

Penny didn't know what to say, so Dan thanked her for getting everyone out safely. He told her to get some rest.

"I'll help Kate," she said, and turned away.

He turned to Neil and Lexi. "Neil, can you get set up with the GPMG? Take some goggles." Neil nodded and turned away towards the munitions trailer. Jimmy was loitering, but Dan waved him away for now.

Dan took Lexi by the arm and walked her away. He stopped and turned her around. "Thank you. You saved the lives of three people by taking that shot. You did the right thing," he said softly.

"I know," she said, looking at the floor. "I-I killed someone, though."

Dan didn't know the best way to deal with this. If he knew her better, he would know how to approach it. He decided on the hard line. "Yes. You did what is expected of you to keep these people safe. You have the skills I need, WE need, to make this work," he said harshly. "You'll find a way to cope with what you did, but I tell you now it was the right thing. Get yourself squared away, reload, and grab a warm coat. I need you ready in five minutes."

He worried that he'd been overly harsh, but didn't have time to talk her through the psychological process of coming to terms with taking a life.

He grabbed his own coat, a foam bedding roll, and his small rucksack. He walked up the drive to a small copse of trees to find Neil setting up under the leaves, the bipod on the barrel of the huge machine gun pointing towards the approach road. Neil also had a shotgun and his Glock and was fitting batteries into a set of night-vision goggles. A curt nod was all Dan got.

"Mate, there aren't enough of us to take it in shifts. We're all going to stay awake tonight," Dan said, knowing it was the wrong way to do it, but he had no choice.

"I can help," said Jimmy, approaching from behind. Jimmy handed a multipack of energy drink cans to Dan and another to Neil.

"I can set up a noise trap," he said. "I saw it in a film – empty bottles and string."

Dan thought about it for a minute. "OK, grab the stuff you need and I'll come with you," he said.

Jimmy ran off and Lexi came jogging towards them.

"Ready," she declared. She saw that both Neil and Dan had a foam roll, and cursed herself silently for not bringing insulation to lie on.

"Lex, I have an idea. Grab your sleeping bag, rucksack, and a bedroll — there's a spare in the back of my truck. I want you set up over there." He pointed towards a small low structure — probably something to do with electricity — with a flat roof which lay about one hundred metres away from where the broken barrier lay at an oblique angle. "You can cover both approach roads from there. It'll be an uncomfortable night, but if you see anyone who isn't friendly, you shoot. Got it?"

She nodded and jogged off to get set up for the night.

Jimmy returned with some string and a crate of small beer bottles. Dan covered him while he tied the string between trees and emptied out the bottles to line them in the road and tie others into the web he had strung. When he had finished, a distorted spider's web of string obstructed the road with small glass alarms dangling from the lines. It would be hard to see in the dark, but anyone running into it would cause the bottles to fall to the tarmac.

Dan thanked him and sent him back to get some rest. Jimmy tried to argue, but Dan told him he needed him as fresh as possible for a nasty job tomorrow. Jimmy went, and Dan jogged across the field to Lexi's position. She had done well. She'd taken a camouflage net from the side of the trailer and was lying flat on the building in her sleeping bag under a crude but effective shelter. She had her rifle trained on the roads.

"If you hear glass breaking, it's the noise traps Jimmy just set up. If they come, I'll try to light them up with flares for you," he said, looking over her hide and giving her the sugary drinks Jimmy had given him. "I'm sure they haven't followed us, but we need to be ready tonight." He considered instructing her in using the night-vision goggles, but decided it wouldn't be effective if she didn't know how they worked.

Dan walked back towards Neil and found him settled in. He told him of the plan to throw some flares if anyone came in, which would give them light. His plan was risky because he was close to Neil's field of fire, and would be in Lexi's if she fired to the left side of her field.

He set up in a shallow dip behind an oak tree, which was almost as wide as his Defender, for a little more security; Neil's weapon could bring a brick-built house down with a thousand rounds and the tree wouldn't hold out forever, but this was the best he could do. He needed to be close enough to hear the glass breaking and throw the few flares he had onto the road if they came. He settled down on his bedroll, rested the carbine over his rucksack, and, like all the others there, he didn't sleep at all.

CALM AFTER THE STORM

As day broke, Dan shuffled backwards from his hiding place, gathered his gear, and walked a long loop back down to the road, stretching his cramped muscles as he went. He lit a cigarette, having refrained from smoking all night to avoid giving away his position. Hard Routine.

Neil looked awful, but he was still awake. Dan told him to stow the machine gun but keep the shotgun with him. He walked over to Lexi's hiding place and found her asleep face down on the bedroll.

He called her name softly as he approached, not wanting to startle a scared, tired, and emotionally unstable girl holding an automatic weapon. She came round with a yelp and brought the weapon up, searching for a target.

"It's OK," he said. "It's me. We're safe."

Lexi breathed hard for a few seconds before struggling out of her hide and starting to take it down.

He walked with her back to the makeshift camp to find people emerging from the wobbling caravans. It didn't look like anyone had slept.

He knocked and stepped into the ambulance where Kate woke with a start from the seat she was slumped in. She had worked tirelessly on the man, and Dan could see dressings covering the exposed parts of the machete victim. He was attached to a drip and was still unconscious. Dan nodded to Kate, who stood and stretched before checking the man over again.

Dan could hear the sounds of a camp kettle being lit, and realised he was in desperate need of a coffee.

He met Neil at the back of his trailer and thanked him for last night.

"Scary shit, mate," Neil said with a sigh of relief. "Think they made us?"

"No," Dan replied. "They would've been on us like a rash if they had. They didn't strike me as the recce-and-dawn-raid kind of people."

He did the rounds, accepting thanks and hugs from others. They were all frazzled, but a sense of relief was starting to wake them up – they had survived their flight. He found Maggie leading the girl out of their caravan.

She saw Dan and led the girl gently towards him.

"This is Alice. Her dad is called Mike. I'll tell you the rest later," she said quietly. Alice looked at him; he decided her face said *thank you* and he didn't push for anything more.

"Your dad is alive. Kate worked on him all night, by the look of it. He's lost a lot of blood, but –" He stopped, not wanting to say that he might pull through.

Maggie led Alice over to the ambulance, where she stared blankly at her father.

Dan called everyone together and accepted a cup of coffee from an unusually dishevelled Penny.

"I'm sure we weren't followed," he announced loudly. "We've put well over ten miles between us and them, and I think they were scouting far from home to be where we were." That got some nervous smiles and nods. "I wanted to do this with a little more ceremony, but welcome to our new home," he said as he gestured towards the ornate front of the big manor house. "That said," he continued, "we have a lot of work to do before we can move in. It's something of a fixer-upper."

"In need of modernisation?" asked Neil, attempting to lighten the mood.

"Something like that," Dan replied with a tired smile. "I need every adult male – sorry ladies, this is no time to claim sexism or shout about equality," he said, holding a hand up to ward off the protests, "to be ready for some dirty work as soon as we've eaten. Ladies, don't think there will be easy work for you; you will need to keep an eye out while we're inside."

Dan walked to the area to the side of the main entrance where the lorries were abandoned. This part was more modern than the old building, a modern attachment to accept large deliveries into the kitchens and stores. He went into the building and opened a cleaning store. He found cleaning products, but not the kind of protective gear he wanted. He thought the farm would provide that.

He walked up, asking Jimmy to come with him. Neil followed with a starter pack, reading his mind again.

"We left our tipper truck, so I'm guessing we need a replacement to move the bodies," Neil said.

"We do, thanks. You should get some rest first, though," said Dan.

"I will," Neil replied. "When you do."

As Neil got a tractor started, luckily still attached to a large trailer, Jimmy helped Dan load up some rubber overalls and wellington boots. A box of paper face masks was in the room, so they came too. They only had three gas masks.

"Mate," said Jimmy. "Can I ask a favour?"

"You want me to say that Kev doesn't have to help," said Dan.

Jimmy looked relieved. "Yeah, please, it's just that he gets scared by dead people a bit and I don't want him freaking out."

"I know. When I said 'adult' males, I was leaving Kev out in my head. I wouldn't expect a young kid to do it, and Kev's in that boat in this sense," he replied.

They sat in the muddy trailer on the short ride down to the house, and Neil parked it directly in front of the main doors.

After a mixed breakfast of whatever they had in their personal kits and cars, Dan took his recruits to the tractor. He had left Penny with a shotgun and offered a weapon to Kate. She flatly refused, saying that she had enough injuries to deal with without causing more.

Dan stood there with Neil, Jimmy, Cedric, Adam, Ian, Kyle – who looked pale – Andrew, and Jay. To everyone's surprise, Liam wandered up in silence to join them.

"Right, this isn't going to be pleasant, but it has to be done. Pair off and get some protective gear on. We carry them out, clearing rooms from the front door in, put them in the trailer, and when it's full, we drive it to the tennis courts and start a fire."

Neil helpfully raised a jerrycan of petrol to underline the point.

"When we think it's clear, we search again. When we're absolutely sure, we bleach and scrub where the bodies were. Lots of them are in bed, so carry them out on the mattresses with the bedding and burn the lot. Open the windows as we go. The quicker we work, the quicker we are done."

They worked quickly. In some areas, the smell wasn't too bad, but in others it was stomach-churning. Dan dragged out large buckets, mops, and stiff brushes. He poured bleach liberally into the buckets and asked Liam to fetch bottles of water. The trailer filled quickly, and he called a break for everyone as he and Neil rode down to the tennis courts. Dan sat on the tool box as he rode up front with Neil, not wanting to share the trailer with the rotting load. The gas masks had left deep red lines in their faces. The trailer was backed in, straight through the fence and felling a section of it, and the two set to work unceremoniously dumping the former inhabitants of their new home to the concrete.

"Still a bloody drain on the working man," Neil quipped about the now dead former guests of Her Majesty. Dan was too tired to respond.

They decided to wait to set the flame until all the bodies were out, and rode the tractor back to the house. The others were nowhere to be seen, so they went inside to find a large pile of bodies wrapped in blankets and resting on thin single mattresses in the atrium. They must have decided not to enjoy their break and just get it done. Later, it turned out that Jimmy had shamed them all by pointing out that the only two people not taking a break were the ones who had been up all night keeping watch over them.

Liam was scrubbing at the floor where the dead prison officer had sat; the chair he had occupied was by the pile for burning.

They repeated this twice more, until the pile was sickeningly high. Dan called a forced break and suggested lunch, but nobody had the stomach for food. He felt a little callous, but ate a nutty chocolate bar despite the pale looks he received. Truth was, he felt dead on his feet. The adrenaline of the shooting, the panicked flight, and a night spent cold, cramped, and on edge had taken a toll on him physically and mentally.

Dan reckoned one more trip would finish it.

Liam struggled with the weight of carrying bodies, and by the look of him had also been sick, so he had busied himself to the result that the place smelled of bleach – like a swimming pool with too much chlorine in. Bleach was good; bleach killed bacteria from dead people. Bleach didn't smell like rotten guts.

By late afternoon, the last trailer was loaded, and before Dan and Neil set off to burn the bodies, he called out to his sweaty, tired group. "Thank you. This was hard work that will haunt us for a long time, but it's nearly done. We can have a proper roof over our heads tonight. Please make another search of every room, every cupboard, and make sure we haven't missed anything. Open all the windows you can find, and help Liam get the cleaning done. Neil and I will go and get the bodies from the gym and be back after."

Neil and Dan rode the tractor again, carried the men from the gym, and went back for the chairs the bodies had leaked into in the week since they had last sat down. All of it went onto the bonfire, and Neil stood on the rear of the trailer for added height to pour twenty litres of petrol over the foul pile. It looked like pictures he had seen of mass graves following some foreign genocide.

They stood well clear and stripped off their overalls, adding them to the pile. Dan lit a smoke and the two just stood in silence for a while. He took another cigarette, lit it from the last one, and threw the red-hot end towards a creeping tendril of petrol heading in his direction.

Even from ten metres away, the *whoomph* of the petrol catching sent a shockwave out. The fire caught quickly, and neither had the stomach to wait for the sizzling and crackling of burning humans.

The tractor was driven back to the house, where it was parked ready for any more rubbish to be piled into for burning.

Dan strolled in to the house. The smell of bleach was thick in his throat, and he reassessed whether he should move people in tonight. He decided to ask Kate, who said that they should let the place air overnight. The term *off-gassing* leapt into his mind, from a life left far behind.

The workers were subdued as they stripped and washed behind one of the lorries, a thought by Penny who had been boiling water for hours and emptying it into a large plastic bin with a whole bottle of shower gel. Towels had been brought out of the house, small green ones that didn't seem to do much in the way of drying them. Dan certainly felt the cloying stink of bodies still clung to him.

Food was cooked, and Dan ate hungrily. He had barely slept or even closed his eyes in thirty-six hours, and he was starting to feel it. He was worrying that he would have to organise a watch again for the night, and looked around for Lexi. He realised she wasn't with the group.

Penny saw him looking and said, "I sent her to sleep for the day. She'll watch tonight."

Dan was pleased; he would've sorted exactly that if he hadn't been so tired. He finished his food and found Lexi kitting up for the night. She had dressed warmly and was struggling to loosen her body armour to fit over her coat. He helped her and had a thought. He unlocked his trailer and searched the box of attachments for the M4s. He found what he hoped was in there: a passive night scope that didn't require batteries. It amplified ambient light, not as bright as the green glow of the goggles, but it would give her an advantage. She set herself up where Neil had been the night before and told Dan to get some rest.

"I've got this. You need to sleep," she instructed him firmly but kindly.

Utterly exhausted, he crawled into his sleeping bag, stretched out in the back of the Land Rover, and slept.

NEW PLAN

Dan slept until he heard the door of the Land Rover being opened. Neil greeted him with coffee, and was awkwardly offering him one of his own cigarettes.

He shuffled in his sleeping bag towards the tailgate and sat, rubbing his eyes. He took a gulp of the coffee and lit the cigarette. A few more seconds passed before he could make words. "Breakfast?" he asked.

Neil laughed. "I had mine about five hours ago, boyo!" he boomed in a Welsh valleys accent. Dan was confused. "Lunch will be in about half an hour, mate. Nobody wanted to wake you, so I got volunteered because they all thought I was the least likely person to get shot."

Dan took a moment to process that; he'd slept from dusk until lunchtime without stirring. He felt guilty, and also worried that things needed doing and the group would have wasted a morning without direction.

He needn't have worried. Penny had roused them all in silence at breakfast, and they had agreed quietly to leave Dan where he was. Neil was up, a little tired but functioning, and Lexi returned reporting a quiet night. She went to get her head down for a few hours and was still up before him.

Penny had deployed the girls into the house to start emptying, cleaning, and occupying rooms. Already the trailer was full of bedding and rubbish that needed taking to the still-smouldering bonfire that Dan could smell. The men had been set to emptying the stores onto the shelves in the small warehouse attached to the kitchens, the bedding and clothing having been removed to a room in the house and laid on tables in approximate size order. By the time Dan finished his caffeine and nicotine wake-up and slid his feet into his boots, the second of the three small lorries was almost empty.

Penny breezed him along with her for a tour, starting as they entered the main door. "Your offices," she said, indicating the security office on their right.

Dan thought this was a good idea, with maps on the wall and tasks/targets on the whiteboard. There was also a large cupboard at the far end with a sturdy, lockable door; that had to be better than keeping an alarming amount of weaponry in the trailer. He realised with a flash of excitement that he hadn't even had a chance to check the full contents yet.

They walked through to the main reception area, which had been used as a temporary storage site for bags and boxes, then through to a large canteen complete with hot plate serveries. Already plans were being made to bring in one of the gas hob cookers, as the kitchen was lacking in natural light – better to not use all their fuel on running generators – and gas tanks were in good supply if you went to the right places.

They went through the kitchen – well stocked with large pots and pans – and into the stores area. Dan was impressed that they had enough food and water to last a few weeks and plenty of space for more stock.

Back inside, Penny led him upstairs. "Single men," she announced, pointing to a large dormitory where Kyle and Liam were looking through and clearing away the personal effects of the previous occupants. There were eight single beds and accompanying large lockers. "Smaller dormitories have been kept aside for married couples." She indicated a room where Maggie was arranging two single beds to make one double.

Dan noticed curious marks on the floor and realised that someone must have used a heavy socket and wrench set to take out the large bolts holding it down. He thought that the new occupants were trusted not to use the beds as barricades, unlike the previous tenants.

At the very opposite end of the corridor, Penny had placed the single females, pointing out that she added herself to this category for now to ensure proper behaviour. The room was being similarly sorted by a few of the girls.

He was happy to see Alice sitting on the bed with Leah while she folded clothes into bags for disposal. She seemed better, no longer catatonic with fear.

Other rooms were left as they were, as they weren't in need of the space.

Yet, Dan hoped.

"I hope you don't mind me setting myself apart, Penny," he said, "but I'd like to find some quarters closer to the front door."

Penny didn't object. "There is a similar-sized office opposite your new operations centre. Perhaps you could take residence in there, if you wished?"

Dan thanked her and said he'd check it out. *Operations Centre*, he thought with a chuckle to himself; Penny did love to give formal titles to everyone and everything. He'd probably wake up to a carved plaque outside his door indicating the primary residence of the First Ranger.

Dan walked back to the main reception room with Penny and was shown through to a nurses' office. Kate had wasted no time at all, and had already set up a field hospital and had started to turn the waiting area into a ward. Boxes and boxes of looted medication were waiting to be sorted and stored. Kate was tending to Mike, who had been moved inside on the ambulance stretcher. He was propped up and awake. Kate was feeding him sips of what smelled like soup.

Mental note: A few beds need to be brought to our new hospital suite.

Kate smiled when she saw them, and introduced them.

"Mike, this is Dan, the one who found you and Alice and brought you back," she beamed proudly.

Mike's eyes glazed a little, but he tried his hardest to straighten up and offer a firm hand to Dan. He was desperately weak and clearly in lots of pain. Kate had spent all night gluing and binding his wounds. He really needed stitches, but what little suture equipment Kate had already found was not enough. Mike was going to have a lot of scars, but he and Alice were alive.

"Thank you," Mike croaked as he winced and shook Dan's hand. He repeated it again three times and just didn't know what else to say yet.

"Rest now, Mike," Kate said, and turned to Dan. "I've given him pain meds which should knock him out soon. He needs to stay in here for probably a week until he can move."

Dan nodded at her and asked if she needed help.

"Not yet, but if you find a surgeon or another paramedic or a GP or a long-legged blonde model, then *please* bring them to me. Gagged and bound if needs be!" she said with a crooked smile.

Dan laughed and promised to do that. He noticed how Penny was perplexed by the blonde model comment, but she was too polite to allow herself to ask.

He opened the door to what would be his own room, and found it full of boxes. He pulled them out and opened them using his knife, finding brand-new quilted blankets. He grabbed the next two people to walk past – Adam and Cedric – and asked them to pile the bedding in the reception room as he opened the rest of the boxes to check the contents. The blankets would need to go into a bedroom somewhere, and the boxes would be useful for scavenging.

Once his room was empty, he sorted out the few bits of furniture. The large office desk and chair were pushed into the corner to give more floor space, and he brought in his own kit from the Land Rover. He had two large sash windows that could be opened up to almost head height – useful for defence. And smoking.

He set up his camp cot, not having the energy to find a metal-framed bed and carry it down, threw down his roll mat and sleeping bag before adding a couple of the new blankets to the pile.

Dan opened the cupboards and removed armfuls of ring binders containing reports on inmate activity and working hours. Useful firelighters for the future, but the folders would be useful to compile reports in his "operations centre." He chuckled again at himself; he was starting to be infected by Penny's terminology.

His spare clothes were stacked onto the shelves, along with toiletries and water. Two bottles of single malt were tucked in there too, along with numerous cartons of cigarettes. He walked through to the office opposite, and started to pull down all the posters and notices, piling them on the central desk. All the CCTV monitors were useless, but removing them was more hassle than it was worth, and besides, they may find someone who could get them working again. All the paper went outside onto the rubbish trailer, which gave Dan an involuntary shudder when he remembered the last cargo he had moved with it. The cupboard was emptied and the other bunches of keys that could open it were locked inside.

He looked around for either Neil or Lexi, but couldn't see either. Everyone was busy working on something under Penny's instruction, so he carefully carried every item from his trailer into the new armoury.

He rested all the long weapons against the wall and organised ammunition, attachments, cleaning equipment, and other goodies on the shelves above.

He laid out the five ownerless Sig 9mm pistols on a shelf directly in front, with the boxes of appropriate ammo and spare magazines to the side. He wanted nothing more than to find another few people that he could trust to carry these. He decided to strip and clean his weapons and relax the magazines, which occupied him for twenty minutes and allowed him some time to think. He left the carbine and his body armour on his bed, tucking the Sig into his waistband in the small of his back and putting a spare mag in the left leg pocket of his combat trousers. Already he felt safer and more relaxed.

He did the rounds of all the rooms again, talking with people as he went. Jimmy and Kev were busy sorting the stores out with Andrew. Things were being placed on the right shelves for easy access: short dates at the front and longer dates at the back. Kev seemed happy lugging boxes and bags full of looted stuff from the lorries, as did Ian.

Andrew was sorting toiletries and non-food stores into a separate pile, and Dan saw Adam and Jay walk in, pick up a box each, and disappear back into the house. Shortly after, Liam walked past carrying large bags of unwanted contents from the rooms towards the trailer. An effective machine was turning, and Dan realised he had had very little to do with it.

He walked back outside and lit a cigarette as he wandered round to the side where he heard noises. He found Neil busily setting up four generators on pallets to keep them off the floor. Neil was hammering long nails into more pallets to create a kind of box to protect them. He saw Dan and gestured towards the pile of heavy canvas tarpaulins.

"Gotta keep these babies healthy," he said. Jerrycans were lined up to the side, marked with green stripes of spray paint, and wires were coming from the back in a series of snakes. Neil's Land Rover had been turned into a kind of mobile workshop, and the back was full of tools.

"I've been up the farm," he said. "Ana's there seeing to the animals and stuff." He saw Dan's face and raised a hand to calm him. "Lexi is with her."

He didn't voice his now void argument, and Neil continued, "Red diesel tank up there, half full. I've topped off the 4x4s and trucks from our tanker and emptied the rest into the farm tank. It's still not full," he said with a smile, which Dan took to mean that they had lots of diesel.

"I've rigged a hand pump to it and knocked off the locks, but just make sure you hang up the hose after you use it!" Neil seemed pleased with himself.

"Nice work, mate," said Dan. "What's the best way to fill it up again, then?"

Neil gestured for him to walk to the tanker. Dan saw that the smallest generator had been securely attached to the chassis of the trailer using a series of lorry straps. It seemed that Neil had rigged his pump system to go mobile now – all they had to do was remove the locks to petrol-station reservoir tanks, drop in the hose, and pump it all out into the tanker. Neil also showed Dan the two hand pumps he had constructed to siphon petrol separately for the generators.

"I'm impressed!" said Dan sincerely. "I don't know if we should use all our fuel keeping the lights on here, though."

Neil agreed, but wanted the electricity supply to be ready for when it was needed.

Dan lit another cigarette, slapped Neil on the back, and wandered towards the house. He sat in the office. He couldn't refer to it as "Operations" without feeling ridiculous, and he picked up pen and paper. He started to write a list of priority supplies to get their new home up and running: chemical toilets, as they had lost theirs when they fled in the night; gas tanks for cooking; more fuel; medical supplies – Kate needed to be escorted to a hospital to scavenge as much as possible. Bedding too, though not really a priority, but all the quilts and pillows they could find would be nicer than prison blankets. They would also need clothing and boots in all sizes.

Food wasn't really an issue, as they had brought plenty, not counting the commercial stores they found at the prison. There was also still fresh meat there, as the freezers were sealed tight so they were good enough to keep things cold and fresh without electricity.

Getting the creature comforts right was important. He thought of a mass shopping trip the next day, vowing to only scavenge to the north for the foreseeable future. He remembered the commercial van lot he'd found with Leah, and decided to stop off there for a couple of vans.

The plan formed in his head, poured out onto his paper, and was rewritten twice over. He planned on taking most of the group with him tomorrow for a fire sale: Everything must go. Three full lorries, a few full vans, trailers… One big hit that should set them up for a while without having to leave home.

Well, Dan would, but the majority could stay and settle. He looked up to see Lexi walking in with Ana. He waved Lexi in and mockingly introduced her to the "Ops Centre." She gave him a puzzled look but sat down with him anyway. He suggested she relax her magazines and clean her weapons, which she did under instruction. She shut her rifle and body armour into the cupboard and kept the Glock with her as Dan had with his Sig. He told her of his plans for tomorrow and showed her a few locations on a map.

He took Penny aside before they all sat down at an actual table and ate using cutlery. It was plastic cutlery, but it still felt more civilised. The only people not present were Kate, Alice, and Mike, who were eating in the medical unit.

Penny agreed to let Dan take the lead on issuing tomorrow's orders, and after dinner, he called everyone to listen up.

"Excellent work, everyone. This place is looking good already, and we can make it great. I've planned a big trip tomorrow, and everyone has a part to play. We will be heading north and taking the three lorries, my Defender, Neil's Defender with the tanker, Lexi's Defender, which was Andrew's previously, and Cedric's Disco. We've already found one large trailer which Cedric is taking to do his thing with the chemical toilets again. Here is the plan," he said, and everyone leaned in to listen.

"Jimmy and Kev, you'll take your truck and go with Neil to a supermarket which I will lead you to. Neil, you fill the tanker with diesel and the jerrycans with petrol while Jimmy and Kev empty the shop of water and supplies. Help them load when you are finished with the fuel and return here after." Nods from Jimmy and Neil, and a smile from Kev, who was pleased to have been named.

"You are getting some food and water, but also quilts and pillows and toiletries. Empty the pharmacy while you're there." Agreement again.

"Once I've pointed out the shop to you, I'll continue on taking Andrew and Ian in my Defender. Lexi will be in the other Defender, followed by Adam and Kyle in another of the trucks." Nods again from those named. "Jay and Liam in the last one." Liam looked surprised to have been involved, and hadn't been paying too much attention until then.

"You will be followed by Cedric and Maggie in their Disco and trailer." Firm nod of agreement from Cedric; Maggie just smiled at him and leaned in to touch her forehead to his in a loving gesture of intimacy.

"Lex will lead you to a large camping shop. She will clear the building first, then Cedric will load the chemical-toilet supplies. Adam and Kyle will collect all the gas bottles you can find, including the camping gas stuff from inside, and Jay? Liam?" He looked at them, getting eager looks in return.

"You will take all the clothing, bags, and boots from the shop. *Everything*," Dan emphasised.

"Andrew and Ian, you'll pick up large vans from a place I found and follow me to where Ian used to work. You'll load your vans with solar panels for future use." Dan decided it was best to recover those first and store them until they could be used. "I'll run protection for you, Lexi for those at the camping shop, and Neil for Jimmy and Kev."

Still nobody spoke; he wasn't sure whether this was tiredness or apathy. He hoped tiredness.

"Penny and Ana will stay here to help Kate look after Mike and Alice." Silent agreement from Penny and Ana. Dan knew he had left Leah out, and knew that she would be fuming about this, so he threw in his final instructions just as she was opening her mouth to protest.

"Leah will also stay here and man the operations centre," he said, managing to keep a straight face. "We need detailed records of who left at what time in what vehicle. We then need to know who returned when, in what vehicle, and what their cargo was. Can you keep on top of that for a whole day?" he kindly challenged her.

Leah tried her hardest to play it cool, but the baited hook had been taken. "You got it," she said along with a sarcastically lazy salute.

They had their orders; nobody had questioned them. They cleared their plates into a large sink to soak with cold water and washing-up liquid – much easier to do that and just wipe them off after. The end of the world had relaxed the washing-up standards, it seemed.

Some people drifted off to their own thoughts as the light started to fade. Some went into what had been named the lounge and which had a large but useless TV and some half-comfortable chairs. Some had found books from the library. Cedric and Neil started to play cards. Dan wandered outside for a smoke. He was joined by Lexi.

"Got a spare one of those?" she asked. He had thousands of them, for now. He reached into his right leg pocket and pulled out the pack and lighter, handing them to her silently. She took one, lit it, inhaled slowly, and a small cough escaped her.

"Never had you down as the menthol type," she said, amused.

Dan noticed how she pocketed the rest of the pack and his lighter. He used to know a woman who did that to him all the time.

"Lex, I know I'm asking a lot of you, but –"

"Don't worry about it," she said, interrupting. "I've got your back. Besides, Penny gave me the speech earlier about the First Ranger not having to take on every dangerous task." She invested his unwanted title with a touch of humour, and the two lapsed into silence, standing in the darkening shadow of the ornate entrance.

Lexi dropped her cigarette butt and ground it out with her boot. "Night, Stark," she said, proud of her comedic timing as she walked inside.

He didn't have the heart to call after her that Neil had used that joke days before.

EVERYTHING MUST GO

An early rise for everyone was attributed entirely to Penny's loud "assembly" voice, which she had only previously used to silence a large crowd of bored children.

Dan rolled out of his cot, had a shower in a can, and dressed in yesterday's combats and top before wandering outside to brush his teeth. He went into the canteen, which was now being called the dining room by Penny, and saw a strange version of a hotel continental breakfast.

There were plates and bowls lined out, boxes of breakfast biscuits, a fruit salad, tea and coffee, and fruit juices. There was bacon and eggs too, which Dan never got bored of. He washed down three cups of coffee and went to get himself sorted out.

An air of expectation was hanging over the group, like a sense of urgency or purpose invaded their thoughts. Everyone was moving that little bit quicker today.

"Morning, boss," called Jimmy cheerfully from the reception room. Kev, as ever, was just behind him. "Bit of a problem with Kyle this morning," he said. "Decided he wanted to stay in bed because he felt poorly…"

Dan realised there was more to the story, so he played along. "Oh? And where is Kyle now?" he asked innocently.

"Outside waiting to go. I promised him he could stay in bed as long as Kev and me could get in with him. I also told him the story of the last people who didn't pull their weight in this group. Seemed to make him feel better all of a sudden."

Dan laughed and slapped his hand on Jimmy's shoulder as he walked to his room.

Dan put on his body armour, tightened it, and checked his magazines. The Sig went back into the chest holster. He packed his small day bag with his trauma kit and emergency rations, then walked through to the office where he found Leah sitting at the big desk looking over the map with a pile of snacks and bottles of juice nearby. She looked very serious. Lexi was leaning against the wall by the armoury, which he unlocked.

They took their respective weapons, and Dan took the tactical shotguns and two belts of cartridges too: one for Neil and one for Penny. He had agreed this with Penny last night – any sign of trouble, they were to barricade themselves inside the medical wing and sit tight until he returned. The shotgun was a small insurance policy for her which he insisted she agree to, despite her being quite sure that nothing of the sort would happen.

He ran through the four locations on the map with Leah. She had found sticky coloured labels and was marking them one to four as he spoke.

"Here is the supermarket and fuel station," he pointed to the map, "where Neil, Jimmy, and Kev will be going. Here is the van place we found," he said, using a pen to pinpoint the small lot. "Here is where Ian used to work, and here," he moved his finger a long way to the side, "is where Lexi is taking the rest."

Leah understood, stuck her different-coloured dots down, and went to the whiteboard, where she wrote locations and names corresponding to the four locations. Dan thought that was pretty impressive, and showed her more.

"This is where we are now," he said, using a red pen to draw around the grounds of the prison and farm. As he did so, his gaze lingered on a lot of farms and open land in the area and made a mental note to search them.

"This is where we were," he said, pointing to Morrisons. He drew a red line there, cutting off the bottom bit of the map and saying, "That's out of bounds until we know more."

"Got it," Leah said.

She would happily sit there with her music and snacks all day, he thought. He went outside and tossed the shotgun and belt to Neil. Very *Bad Boys*, he thought, instantly feeling like a bit of a dick.

Everyone had gathered, forming their convoys. Nothing much was left to say, so Dan stood by his Land Rover and called out to them, "You all know what to do. Be safe, be lucky, and see you all for dinner." With that, he climbed in and started the engine.

They drove in a long convoy of four off-road vehicles, two towing trailers, and three lorries. When they reached a roundabout probably two miles away, Lexi peeled off to the right followed by Cedric's Discovery and two of the trucks. Neil was behind with his Defender and tanker, with Jimmy and Kev in the remaining truck behind.

When they reached the large roundabout where the supermarket was, Dan waved them off through his open window, leaving just him, Andrew, and Ian in his own vehicle. Andrew was sitting in the back;

he took this position almost naturally as a submissive kind of person. Dan thought there probably wasn't a single trace of alpha male gene in his body, but felt that he was clever and well organised, which compensated.

They reached the van sales lot, and Dan found the keys to two long-wheelbase, high-sided vans. Both were fuelled enough to not have to use the jerrycans from his Land Rover, and Ian took the lead to where he used to make deliveries. The journey took nearly forty-five minutes, but Dan realised they may have found something very important when they turned in. After a quick look around, they decided to ditch the new vans and take the ten-ton lorry which was already loaded with solar panels and various pipes. It was easier to store it as it was and just park the lorry somewhere rather than mess around moving it.

Ian drove and Andrew went with him. As agreed, when they got close to home, Dan would peel off and make use of the rest of the day. They were told to find somewhere to park the lorry that wouldn't cause an issue and report to Leah with their haul.

Dan spun around at the island where they had first split off from Lexi's. He decided to leave Neil's and Lexi's groups alone, and allow them to form their own leadership status without him interfering. He decided to head in the direction between where Neil had gone and where Lexi was, which led to a small town probably thirty miles from home. He rolled through slowly, looking from side to side as he crawled.

He couldn't see anyone, but he had an unmistakable sense of being watched. He decided to stop and have a break, to see if anyone would creep out from the woodwork. He sat on his bonnet with a coffee and lit a cigarette, being careful to give off the *not a care in the world* vibe when in fact he was acutely tuned in to every sound.

He sat there, sipping his coffee and smoking, with his feet on the winch cable and bumper. His M4 hung down between his legs, the suppressor lightly knocking into the grill when he moved. He was certain he was being watched, but decided that scanning the area was probably a bad idea. He didn't want to scare anyone else. He decided to take some action, but nothing that would get him shot at. He threw down his cigarette end, tipped the dregs of his coffee, and jumped to the ground.

"I know you're out there," he called out. "I'm alone and I'm friendly." He left it at that, screwing the cup back onto his metal flask.

Just as he was about to give up, a movement to his left showed momentarily. He turned slowly to see a woman carrying shopping bags and looking very unkempt. She had a young girl, probably three or four years old, hiding behind her legs. The woman looked close to tears; she was clearly scared of Dan, but it looked as though she was not going to last long without modern comforts.

"Are you a soldier?" she asked.

He would have placed her at about the same age as Lexi at the oldest, only this woman was painfully thin and looked weak. "Of a sort, yes," he replied. "I come from a group of people. We have a home set up a couple of towns over. Come back with us?"

The woman still shook and looked to the ground, thinking. "My name's Eve," she said with an air of acceptance. "I have no idea about her because she won't speak to me," she said, nudging the child gripping her legs. "I haven't got a clue about kids, but I found her a few days ago and she just followed me," she finished.

Dan thought that this woman would not last long in the current climate. He opened the rear door of his Land Rover and stepped away, allowing them to approach slowly. He decided that these two could be fixed by others in the group, as he doubted he had the patience. The woman climbed in, but the child was too small to reach that high unaided. It hadn't occurred to Eve to help her in. Dan gently picked her up under the arms, and he felt her whole body tense. He reassured her, and placed her feet on the back seats, where she threw herself in towards Eve.

"Did you come with the other soldier?" Eve asked as he climbed back behind the wheel. That made him stop.

"No. Tell me about this other soldier," he said, trying to control his impatience.

"He looked like you, had army stuff on and a gun," she said, frustrating him with her lack of detail.

"Describe him and the gun. What was he driving? How long ago was it?" he said, forcing himself to go slow with this fragile woman.

"Not long before you came, further up the road. He was shorter than you and a bit older, I think. The gun was a machine gun with a big thing on the top." She sketched an outline of a large optic. "And he was driving a Jeep like this."

He swallowed the retort that Jeeps weren't off-roaders, and off-roaders weren't Jeeps. He decided to take a drive down to the far end of town before he turned and got these two back home. From the smell of them, he didn't fancy spending all day in the car. He surreptitiously wound down his window as he drove.

After another hour searching, he saw no sign of anyone. He decided against leaving any clues to their new location.

Dan drove home steadily, getting occasional questions from Eve. He told her how many of them there were, not counting anyone new that the others may bring back that day. He felt a little cruel for thinking it, but he found Eve very annoying.

He stopped a few times to mark places of interest and take notes. *That should keep Leah busy for a while*, he thought.

He was feeling more hopeful as the days went on now, but a glance behind at a grubby child looking straight at him with suspicious eyes gave him a great sadness for those he had lost.

His own daughter and son. Six and three respectively.

He pushed their memories from his mind and concentrated on the road.

"Grant me the serenity," he recited silently to himself.

THE LEXI SHOW

She was nervous. Her life had changed massively almost every day since all this had started. A week later, she was now some kind of soldier with high expectations of her, and a very tough act to follow.

She couldn't work Dan out at all. She tried to emulate his easy authority, to walk in and assess a place quickly before rattling off what everyone should do. The difference was that he was clearly trained, whereas she wasn't. She wanted to ask to work alongside him and learn, but instead she was leading her very first sortie with other people relying on her for protection.

She pulled into the car park by the big camping warehouse. To her left was a fenced yard where all the tents were set up, some already starting to sag with neglect.

She looked at the doors and decided to do what Dan had told her about; she reversed her unfamiliar Land Rover up to the doors and looped the length of chain around the metal handles. She got back in and drove slowly away to take up the slack. When it held tight, she lifted the clutch to gently force them open. It worked nicely, and she got out to see that she had barely done any damage. She looped the chain and stowed it in the back, trying not to look pleased with herself, as she thought the others might not take her seriously.

She moved her vehicle away and instructed the two lorry crews to their tasks: one to cut the lock to the large caged area where the gas bottles were, and the other to wait for her to check the building before they went to clear it. She slung the rifle on her back, as it was too long to use inside. With the Glock in her right hand and a bright LED torch in her left, she edged into the shop. There was no smell, thank God, and she guessed the place was probably locked up over a week ago and nobody ever returned to open up again.

She stalked through the shop, more conscious of the others watching her from the doorway than anyone inside. Trying to look as professional as she could, she searched the shop floor first, then upstairs on the mezzanine, which she had failed to notice and cover as she first entered.

Lastly, she went aisle to aisle in the stock room and out of the fire escape at the rear.

"Clear," she announced loudly with confidence as she strode back through the shop.

They walked in and started taking things from the racks closest to the front door. This would probably take a few hours, she thought as she strode outside and holstered the sidearm, unslung her rifle, and scanned a full 360 degrees.

Adam and Kyle were already busy loading the gas canisters, and she saw Cedric lowering the tailgate of his trailer as Maggie was carrying a large plastic container of some chemicals.

She climbed up to the roof rack of her Land Rover and continued to scan the area.

People spoke in hushed tones to each other as they worked effectively.

After about an hour of seeing the three pairs loading their vehicles, Maggie announced that they had all the chemical-toilet equipment. Lexi thanked her, but Maggie seemed to be waiting for more.

"Can you and Cedric please help Jay and Liam load the clothes and other stuff?" Lexi asked.

They both went without argument and started to load the lorry with armfuls of clothes and boxes of camping gear.

It dawned on her just how much authority she had been given by being made a Ranger. With that authority, however, came the responsibility of knowing what to do to keep them all safe. That knowledge deflated her slightly, and she took another careful scan of the area through her scope.

Adam came up to her after another hour and reported that all the gas bottles were loaded. Kyle kept a sullen silence, and she suspected that he didn't want to be doing much in the way of manual labour. She had thought that of him before Dan had found them. Kyle was a moaner.

She thought for a second before asking, "How much space is left in your truck?" The answer was half. "Back it up next to the doors and help the others load."

Both went to do as she had asked.

After she couldn't sit still any longer, she called the group out, calmly so they didn't think there was anything wrong.

"How are we doing?" she asked with a smile.

"Shop floor is almost cleared," said Maggie. "Just loads of stockroom now."

Lexi looked at the back of the trucks; both were three-quarters full.

"OK, everyone, take a break and get some food and drink. Back to it in half an hour," she said.

Nobody complained, and they took their food and drinks to the grassy picnic area. Lexi didn't know what to do; should she stay and keep watch, or join them? She didn't want to be seen to do nothing and lose their respect. The decision was made for her when Cedric interjected.

"Come and sit with us. You need to eat too." She liked Cedric and Maggie; they were kind and caring. None of the others objected, so Lexi rested her rifle against the side of a picnic table and sat on the grass. She ate an energy bar and drank a fancy bottle of orange and passion fruit flavoured juice.

They talked quietly between themselves. Lexi listened and joined in here and there, but she still felt apart from the group in lots of ways.

The sound of an engine cut over their conversation.

They all looked at Lexi, who without thinking snatched up her rifle and flicked the safety to semiautomatic as she turned to face the access road.

"Inside the shop. Now," she said to everyone, and they ran to obey, all except Cedric, who remained.

"I'll talk to them, you stay hidden," he said.

Lexi hesitated for a second, but decided to go with the plan and moved forward in a crouch to kneel by the corner of her vehicle. She forced herself to breathe deeply, to calm down and face whatever was coming with a clear head.

Cedric's plan was a good one – why show your hand if the other player folds?

The engine note grew louder, but she didn't think it was being driven hard. The wait was excruciating, and Lexi realised she had heard a loud engine from quite a distance. She steadied herself and saw a dark-green pickup drive past.

It stopped, and she saw the reverse lights illuminate.

Shit! Shit! Shit! Calm yourself, she thought.

The pickup drove in slowly, and the driver got out when he saw Cedric standing still by the shop.

"Hello," the man beamed. He was late fifties; a big man but running to fat, he was dressed like a farmer with moleskin trousers over leather boots and a checked shirt on top. He seemed to hold no malice, but Lexi stayed put and watched him over the top of her scope, as the distance was too short to use the magnification.

He walked towards Cedric with his hand extended and announced that he was called Pete.

Cedric responded with his own name and shook the offered hand. Lexi watched for a while longer, unsure if she should reveal herself just yet.

He saw Pete gesture towards the Land Rover as he spoke to Cedric. Lexi's breath caught in her chest, as she didn't know whether she or the vehicle were the subject of discussion.

"It's OK, everyone," called Cedric loudly as the others started to emerge from the shop.

Pete walked back to his pickup and opened the door. Two cocker spaniels, both a glossy chocolate brown, bundled out and ran around the car park with their noses to the floor. On seeing the others, they bounded up to them, eager for fuss.

Lexi slowly stood and started to walk over. Pete feigned surprise, but his eyes said he already knew she was there. She safetied and slung her rifle before taking the offered hand. "Lexi," she said, and Pete smiled at her.

Introductions were made all round, and Pete in turn introduced Dram and Tot, his "girls." On hearing their names, the dogs sat and stared up at Pete with an almost fanatical obedience, waiting for a command.

Pete came and joined them at their picnic tables and the break was resumed. Pete talked about his experience of the last week, and told them that he was a gamekeeper and in honesty hadn't actually realised anything had happened because he went a few days without seeing anyone if he was busy.

He was a big, loud character, and everyone took to him straight away. He had that quickness to smile and tell a joke, no matter how bad it was, and Lexi thought he and Neil would get on well.

It was suggested to Pete that he join them, and he instantly agreed. He said he was going to load his stuff and would be back later. Hands were shaken again, and Pete gave a short whistle to the dogs as he walked back to his pickup. They responded instantly and flew in through the open door. With a kindly wave, Pete reversed out and drove away.

Lexi had some doubts about him. She was worried about his red nose and large belly, believing she recognised the signs of someone who drank every day.

Everyone was left a little shocked but smiling after he left. Lexi decided it was a good time to take charge before Pete came back and captivated them all again.

"Right, let's get these trucks filled before he's back so we can get home," she said. There was again no argument, but she decided to play an extra card.

"Maggie, can you keep watch for a bit and I'll load up?" she said. Maggie looked a little taken aback but agreed. Lexi locked her rifle into the Land Rover, guessing that if Pete had been around here for a week and not run into trouble then the area was likely to be relatively safe. "Shout if you hear or see anything," she called.

She ran in, grabbed an armful of boxed boots, and ran back to load them into the lorry. She worked twice as fast as everyone else just to make a point, and before long, the trucks were full.

They formed up, ready to set off when Pete returned.

After an hour, they were starting to worry a little.

At ninety minutes, Lexi was thinking of calling it quits and wondering how to convince everyone that it was time to go home. It was approaching teatime, and she was nervous that nobody would agree to leave without him. Luckily, the sound of the rough diesel engine hit the edge of her hearing as she was planning how to word her argument.

Pete drove back in, both dogs sitting in the front passenger's seat and the truck bed brimming with bags and equipment. Lexi saw numerous gun slips and fishing gear. She would have to tell Dan straight away if they wanted to keep guns out of people's hands as a rule.

The convoy loaded up, and although they didn't know it, their group had now grown to over twenty.

MOTION LOTION

Neil was very impressed with his contraption.

He had arrived at the shop with Jimmy and Kev, prised open the doors, and searched the place.

Empty, but the smell from the rotting fruit-and-veg and chiller units was rank. The smell was so awful it had graduated to become a taste.

He reckoned that a week ago, just about everyone had gone home sick, and most, nearly all, never left again.

Jimmy and Kev started work straight away and hit the pharmacy before planning to load with water bottles.

Neil went to the fuel station and cut the padlocks from the reservoir top of the diesel tank. He lowered the hose into the tank as far as he could and started the generator. He'd rigged it to power a small pump that he had found on the industrial estate – that seemed like weeks ago now. He heard the sloshing sound and reckoned it would take a long time to pump out the five thousand litres, so he wandered into the shop and selected some snacks to fill the time. He had six empty jerrycans for petrol, and helped himself to the few plastic cans in the shop: green for petrol, black for diesel. He stuck to the established colour code, as he didn't want to mix the fuels, and used a hand pump to work the petrol out and into the cans.

Before long, he was sweating with the effort. He banged the side of the tanker and saw that it would probably take almost an hour to fill it up. He thought it would be safe to pump the petrol despite having an engine running, as the tanker was a little distance away.

He took a short break and drank a warm can of Sprite. Another fifty minutes of pumping petrol out filled the cans, which he stacked into the back of the Land Rover, bar one that he kept back. He watched the diesel pump working, marvelling again at his own ingenuity. A short while later, he lifted the pipe from the reservoir until the fuel in the pipes was pushed through. He killed the generator, sealed the tanker, and secured all the pipes. He topped up the generator, reckoning that pumping the diesel had used about five litres of petrol. He topped the last fuel can up with his hand pump and put it away. Well stocked with motion lotion, he drove slowly back to the front of the shop.

He saw that Jimmy and Kev had worked hard; the lorry was more than halfway full with stacks of quilts and pillows piled on top of heavy bags of medicines. The back was starting to fill with plastic-wrapped crates of water. Neil chipped in and took a trolley to bring more.

Some boxes of tinned food and all the breakfast bars on the shelves saw the truck full. The sliding doors were forced closed again, and the three rested for a little while before heading back.

They reached the prison just over half an hour later, due to Neil's very slow progress with the heavy trailer. They rolled in during the late afternoon to find they were the second lot to return; Andrew and Ian had brought back a lorry full of solar panels an hour before and parked it out of the way behind the house.

Leah bounded out with Penny, Ana, and Alice following. Jimmy took the lorry to the stores bay while Neil backed his tanker into its previous space. He unhitched it and parked in the circular loop near the front door, bringing both weapons with him.

Leah stood impatiently and Neil answered her unasked question: "Five thousand litres of diesel, eighty of petrol," he said as he walked past her, throwing a salute.

Leah pestered Jimmy for the details of their haul, and was told that they'd emptied the pharmacy, got lots of pillows and quilts, and more food and water.

Leah wrote all this down and returned to Ops to consolidate her reports. She asked how much food was left in the shop, and seemed happy to be told "loads" by Neil.

They rested, deciding to wait for the others to return before unloading. Kate emerged from the front door wearing a set of grey prison-issue jogging bottoms and a light-blue T-shirt. She stretched extravagantly and announced that Mike was sleeping again.

Ana and Alice had been helping Penny prepare a meal for that night. Leah had barely left Ops all day. She was still scribbling notes and updating the board, keeping the relevant number up for the site, noting that there was still food and fuel there.

Dan returned a short while later with Eve and the silent girl. Penny took them straight in and went into full-on fuss mode. Kate joined her, and with the help of Ana, the two new arrivals were scrubbed clean and new clothes were found. Eve's physical condition was explained somewhat when she said she was a vegan. Someone used to surviving on prepared salads and vitamin supplements, who was already painfully thin, would not live long in today's world. Eve was dressed similarly to Kate, in a prison tracksuit, and the girl was put in a sweatshirt which was too big for her, as there was nothing else for her to wear. Eve begged for someone to take the girl from her, but she clung on tighter and refused to be moved. She allowed Kate to check her over and both were pronounced healthy, as long as they got fed and rehydrated.

Dan called a small powwow between himself, Jimmy, and Neil, repeating what Eve had said about the "other soldier." None of them knew what it meant definitively, but the thought of another armed man out there served to sober their thoughts.

Just as nerves were starting to fray and Penny was worrying out loud that dinner would spoil, the outstanding convoy returned. The two lorries were reversed in by Jimmy, Cedric brought his trailer to the front door for unloading, and Lexi reverse-parked her Defender in a mimicking pose of Dan's vehicle. The big surprise for the reception committee was the arrival of a dirty and battered green Isuzu pickup. It looked to be a typical farm wagon, the kind of car you used to open gates with and didn't care much for dents. Or yearly MOTs, road tax, or insurance.

The driver was a happy man, and Dan was introduced to him by Cedric.

"Dan, this is Pete. He found us as we were collecting the stuff. Pete, this is Dan." They shook hands. Pete had big hands and a strong grip. He also smelled faintly of Scotch. He was introduced to everyone there, and the names went over his head in a blur of information overload. He gave two short, sharp whistles, and a matching pair of brown cockers flew from his pickup to run excitedly through the group.

Penny insisted that everyone come inside to eat, and Dan lit a smoke as they trailed off. Lexi hung around after they had gone and raised an eyebrow to him.

"You can get your own, you know; they've come down a lot in price recently," he joked, offering her a cigarette.

She took one with a smile and he lit it for her, conscious to keep control of the pack and lighter this time.

"He's got guns in the back. Gamekeeper," she said, blowing smoke up in the air.

He mused on this. The rules were that nobody would carry a weapon without being ratified by him. The man was unlikely to be a danger, as the guns were for hunting, but something in Lexi's tone made him wonder.

"What are you thinking?" he asked her.

"I'm concerned he might be an alcoholic," she said carefully.

"I think you're right, but an alcoholic and a drunk are two different things. Let's see how this pans out, shall we? I'd be happy with some fresh meat on my plate instead of tinned everything for the next few years," he replied. She raised no objection, and he wondered where her fear stemmed from. Perhaps a family member had succumbed to the evil of drink?

"Still," he said, lifting the four gun slips from the back of the pickup, "can't leave these lying around."

They went inside and joined a happy group comprising all of them, as Mike was well enough to walk the short distance to sit up. He had Kate fussing over him so that he didn't open any wounds as he walked, and he was packed off to bed as soon as the meal was finished.

Dan cleaned and stored his weapons along with Pete's, then walked the grounds for a while as the sun fell low in the sky. He took himself off to the makeshift bathroom, where he heated some water and had a strip wash, getting into a set of grey prison jogging bottoms and a vest. He padded back down to his room, carrying his dirty clothes and boots. He only had a few sets of clean trousers left and would have to search through the new apocalyptic clothing range tomorrow.

He lay on his cot for a long time before he heard footsteps outside his door. A gentle knock, followed by another slightly louder one. He wasn't in the mood to talk to anyone, so he ignored it. He heard his name being whispered loudly by Lexi and decided to definitely ignore it.

Not the time to complicate things.

THE WAY OF THINGS

The haul was unloaded the following morning. The toilets were set up in the new male and female bathrooms, the fuel was pumped into the farm tank, and all the vehicles were filled up.

Dan took Pete aside after breakfast. As suspected, he had drunk quite heavily last night and was sipping from a hip flask as they walked around the grounds. The premise of the tour was to ask Pete to start a hunting and fishing programme to provide fresh meat to the group. He was impressed with the grounds, claiming that rabbits and game birds were plentiful. He had the tools and the knowledge, but Dan wanted to know if he could be trusted.

"What do you want to ask me, lad?" said Pete intuitively, saving him the need for a long preamble. Pete's eyes flashed to his left where he had seen his dogs run into a thicket. Two sharp whistles brought them crashing back out again.

Dan stopped and turned to face him, producing a cigarette packet and lighter. He lit up and inhaled deeply, then said to Pete, "I'm concerned about the drink."

Pete sighed.

Dan saw Pete's hand involuntarily flutter towards a pocket where he thought the hip flask was. "Would you think me a fool if I said that I wasn't?" Dan asked seriously.

"Yes, I drink," Pete said. "But I won't be letting you lot down. I'll play my part and I never get nasty with it. Truth is, I've drunk myself stupid nearly every day since this all went to shit."

Dan didn't doubt Pete's sincerity one bit, but experience told him that the drink took over sometimes and the person didn't realise they had a choice. "I want you to stay, Pete. I really do," he said.

"But?" asked Pete, eager to get to the point. He had a feeling of sadness, sure that he would be told to take his leave of the group. He measured the man in front of him and felt a coldness in him; he didn't want to know what it looked like to upset him.

Pete was lonely. He was lonely before the world changed, if he was honest with himself. He wanted to be a part of this badly.

He still had his pride, and he would not beg the man.

"But there are rules…" said Dan. "Weapons will be issued when they are needed, then cleaned and locked away after they've been used. Not negotiable."

Pete was surprised, having convinced himself that he was being exiled. "Sensible. No argument from me."

"The drinking *must* stay under control," Dan continued, pointing a finger at Pete's chest. "I don't want to have to be an arse and lock the booze away."

"OK," Pete said. He wanted to ask how much he was allowed, but didn't think it would make the conversation any more comfortable.

"And you're coming out with me in a bit," Dan finished. Pete gave him a puzzled look. "That truck is a shed. You're getting a new one."

They set off in Dan's Defender. Pete's battered old Isuzu went under a tarpaulin by the ten-ton parked out behind the house. The dogs jumped around the back seat and boot as they drove. The journey took nearly an hour – the closest dealership was in the area he had declared out of bounds – and he went through the now familiar routine of scouting, breaking in, and clearing the building. Dan selected a twin-cab pickup which was to Pete's liking. The keys were found, and a set of spare wheels went in the back; getting new tyres fitted wouldn't be an issue for some time yet.

Dan reasoned that it made more sense to use newer vehicles with common parts – less likely to break down and become a safety issue. It wasn't just because he liked Land Rovers and wanted the group's fleet to look nice and corporate.

Pete's driving was fine. Dan was watching carefully in his mirror, looking for any sign of the alcohol being a problem. He saw none.

When they got back, he saw that the rest had not been idle. Penny conducted a further tour of the house, showing Dan the fully stocked bedding store. He was also shown the toiletries and towels, and the very impressive clothing store. He realised that everyone was wearing new clothes, including the young girl, who still hadn't spoken or left Eve's side. He saw that everything was separated into male and female, and laid out systematically in size order. There was a selection of boots in different sizes too. "Lots more are in the stores," Penny announced.

He saw that the bathrooms had water heaters made from the camping equipment. In the makeshift medical wing, Alice had been busy helping Kate sort and store the medicines recovered on the scavenging trips. Kate said that they had plenty of antibiotics, which she saw as the most important, as infection was more likely to kill someone nowadays.

Alice had perked up significantly, but still seemed quite fragile. It turned out that she had just finished her first year of university, and her skills in IT and mathematics weren't proving to be in demand. Mike was still confined to bed by Kate, with the exception of being allowed to walk the short distance for the evening meal.

"Thank you again," said Mike to Dan. "You saved our lives. I can't think of what they would have done to my Alice if…" He trailed off, and Dan filled the awkward silence. He knew exactly what they would have done to her.

"You're welcome, Mike. Both of you. Rest and get better, then we need to find you something to do," he said.

"I'm an engineer," Mike said quickly. "I was self-employed and doing well. Just bought an Aston Martin, actually," he said, chuckling to himself. How quickly a lifelong dream could be made to feel utterly pointless.

Dan had a thought and asked, "Do you know anything about solar panels?"

"No," he replied. "But you find me a book on it while I'm stuck in here and I can try my best."

"No problem at all," Dan said, patting him gently on the shoulder as he stood to leave. He looked to Kate to say goodbye but she was engrossed in explaining something to Alice.

"There is more," said Penny with a smile. "It appears your new operations coordinator is using her initiative and wants to interview the group. She is plotting scavenging sites on the map as we speak."

Dan was impressed. He walked into Ops and Leah looked up with a grin. She launched straight into an uninvited report on supplies that could be recovered and places she was suggesting for checking.

He saw an old Yellow Pages on the desk next to her notebook. That was probably the most impressive of all: How a child from the Google age could adapt to using the old-fashioned methods. They could all do with a lot more of that.

"I hear you want to interview the others," Dan said seriously. Leah seemed a little put out, having just questioned her plan on hearing his tone.

"I thought people might remember different shops or know about things…" Leah trailed off as he looked directly at her.

He left her in suspense for a few more seconds before he spoke. "Good idea. Can you start after dinner?" She nodded, delighted at the praise.

"Let me know what you find, then we can sit down and prioritise what we need. Remember to take a break, though, kid. OK?" he said as he walked out to hide his proud smile. Leah called out after him that she would, but he doubted it. He was worried that before long, she would want to be taught how to drive and shoot.

Lexi was loitering, and he thought he would probably have to have the difficult conversation soon. He thought it better to do it now, and thanked Penny as he walked outside to smoke.

Lexi joined him very soon after, lighting one of her own. Dan decided to take the professional line before she embarrassed herself.

"I heard your trip went well," he said. "How comfortable are you weapons wise?" he asked.

"OK with the rifle," she replied. "Less so with the Glock. I wasn't too sure about searching the buildings."

"And the driving?" he asked.

"I could do with some pointers on everything," she said, hopeful.

"OK. With me tomorrow, you're driving," he said as he put out his cigarette and went back inside. He thought it was very normal for this kind of thing to happen: People had been through trauma and were scared. Lonely. It was perfectly natural for feelings to manifest, but he wanted to nip it in the bud straight away for a number of reasons: one, he didn't really find her attractive. Not that she was unattractive, just that she wasn't his type. Two, he saw how a couple of the others looked at her, and didn't particularly want to have the group devolve into some sort of stag rutting competition. Better to stop it before it started.

After dinner, Penny announced that everyone should go to the lounge area where Leah had a few questions for them all. Everyone agreed and took part willingly to make Leah happy. She had prepared a list of questions for everyone in her neat handwriting.

Penny called a meeting of senior members: Dan as Head of Operations, Neil as Head of Engineering, Jimmy as Head of Logistics, Andrew as Head of Supplies, and Kate as Head of Medical. Penny was there as Head of "Home," and asked them each in turn to give a rundown of their "staff" as well as needs and suggestions.

Dan started. "Lexi is performing well. I need to take her out tomorrow for some training, but she's doing all right. Leah is doing a great job – she's got more tasks than we have people and storage space."

He finished, nodding to Neil.

"Ian's got a lorry full of solar panels, as you know. Mike reckons he can learn how to fit them. If that happens, I'll need to borrow Adam to do some plumbing work. I'll need logistics to empty the plumbing aisle in B&Q too," said Neil. Nods all round. "Fuel – we've got plenty for now, but everyone should still bring back jerrycans when they see them."

He gestured to Andrew, who said, "Stores are fairly well stocked. We need to future-proof things in terms of growing our own food, but we have maybe three years of living on tins, jars, and bottles if we have to. Any empty space on the lorries should be filled with bottled water." He spoke quietly, nervous at being involved. "Liam is doing well; he's learning how to do the job." He shrugged, with nothing more to add.

Kate was sitting next in line. "I've got plenty of medicines, but I could do with visiting an A&E. It's going to be messy, though; hospitals were overrun and people died in the waiting rooms."

"How about waiting a couple of months?" suggested Dan. "As sick as this sounds to some, it may be better to wait until the bodies have decomposed instead of trying to get in there at the worst time."

"That might be better, actually, but we're talking three months minimum, I reckon," Kate said. Nobody wanted to chip in on that, so Kate continued, "I'd like an escort to the ambulance stations in the interim so I can take the rest of the stores there. Mike is healing well, and I'd say he can move around more in a week or so; some of the cuts were deep, and he should've had more stitches than I could put in."

"What about Alice?" asked Dan.

Kate looked up, surprised at the question, as she didn't know where he was going with it. "She seems a little traumatised, but is doing well now. No injuries."

"Do you think you can teach her basic medical skills?" he asked.

Kate thought for a second before replying, "Yes. I need medical texts, though."

Dan nodded and looked to Jimmy.

"Vehicles are good, people are good – apart from Kyle, who has had to be *encouraged* a few times." He emphasised the word *encouraged*. "I could do with a few more pairs of hands, but that's it."

"Well done, everyone. Our progress is quite *encouraging*," Penny said, making light of Jimmy's jest. "I have taken Eve under my wing, and the child who never leaves her side. She still won't speak to anyone. Eve is... unskilled, shall we say." She hesitated. Dan would have said "useless" but Penny wasn't unkind enough to say so. "I have had to instruct her with cooking and cleaning, but she has some issues with food preparation. We could do with more qualified or experienced people, as I am undertaking the majority of the cooking – I don't have an issue with this, you understand," she added.

They discussed further forays for supplies. Dan would take Lexi out as planned, and Jimmy would deploy two lorries to collect more food and water.

Pete was going to start hunting the next day, and had been helping Ana with the farm. Maggie had suggested that seed packets be recovered for growing vegetables, and she was going to go out with Cedric – inseparable as always.

Neil planned to start sorting out the workshop on the farm and equipping it as a vehicle workshop. Ian would be helping him with that. They had found chainsaws and a log splitter for attaching to the rear of a tractor on the farm, and Jay was nominated to start stacking logs for the coming winter. He had happily agreed to this, and wanted to collect some equipment from his old workplace. Jimmy offered to drop him off there to get his dropside van and tools.

The benefit of the old house was that it had chimneys in many rooms. Liam was nominated to help Jay when he wasn't needed in the stores.

"What about our security concerns?" Penny asked Dan.

"We haven't seen any sign of hostility since we left the supermarket. Everyone knows that the area to the south is effectively out of bounds for now. I'm relaxed enough to allow scavenging without armed support, but everyone must be cautious," Dan said. "Anything people don't like the look of, get out of the area and let me check it out."

Meeting over, they all went with their own thoughts. Jimmy offered his and Kev's help to wash up that night, which Penny graciously accepted.

Dan considered their numbers over a solitary Scotch, musing that they simply did not have enough to survive in the long run.

OLD-FASHIONED BOOKS

"Time and motion, boy," Dan's dad had always told him. He always tried to combine his tasks to maximise efficiency. To that end, he told Lexi to drive to the nearest town centre to find the public library that Leah had found in her Yellow Pages. Lexi drove her Land Rover, asking for and receiving tips on her technique.

"Keep your thumbs outside the wheel," he said at one point. "If you hit a big pothole or something, the wheel can pull and hurt you." She nodded and folded her thumbs on the outside. She scanned as she drove, as she had seen him do.

They arrived at the town centre and drove through slowly. Dan noticed that already the rubbish swirled along and gathered against walls and kerbs. It probably wouldn't be long before nature started taking back what people had taken first, and Dan mused that the roads would degrade fairly quickly too, especially when the weather got bad. Another reason for choosing the best 4x4xfar.

The library was unlocked, and a pull on the door let out a nauseating smell. Dan held up a hand and went back to the Land Rover for his bag. He came back to Lexi with chewing gum and two paper masks. Lexi was puzzled at first, but followed suit and started to chew three pieces behind her mask. It worked, and the smell of rotting body was diluted by mint. As they had agreed, Dan led and Lexi watched. He moved at a slight crouch using his Sig, as Lexi would be using her Glock to do the same job. He cleared the aisles of books, nodding directions to Lexi as he went. They found two bodies, not worth checking for breathing, as they were visibly starting to decompose. The systematic search continued, Lexi copying Dan's movements in silence. He finally holstered the Sig on his chest and turned to her. "Questions?" he asked, trying to keep his tone professional and not encourage intimacy.

"What did you do on the corners?" she asked.

He drew his weapon again and talked her through it. "Approach the corner, take a step out from the wall. Eyes and gun always point the same way. Step around slowly and the blind area will open up. Always keep scanning for any height advantage someone could have over you."

"Got it," she said.

They split up and searched the shelves for manuals and textbooks. They found medical texts, guides on growing crops, and two books on solar panels. Dan wasn't sure if it was the right thing, but it was all they found. Lexi brought back a book on high-frequency radio signals and radio operating. It looked like an old book to Dan, but then again, so was the skill in the modern age of satellites and computers.

With a box of books in the back of the Land Rover, they locked it and took their weapons for a check of the indoor shopping area after using a small pry bar to force the automatic doors. The bar went down the back of Dan's vest in case they needed it again.

The normal shops were all there, shrouded in an eerie sense of emptiness. He held up a hand to stop Lexi, indicating with two fingers pointed at his eyes that she should stay and keep watch. He went into a card shop, returning within thirty seconds. Lexi wanted to ask, but didn't want to look stupid, so she kept quiet. They walked onwards slowly, Lexi trying to impress by showing that she was covering the corners and blind spots.

He felt relatively safe and was happy to watch Lexi demonstrate the skills she was mimicking, skills that he had learned by repetition and constant yelling of "Bang! You're dead!" over and over whenever he got it slightly wrong.

They found a small army surplus shop, one that advertised a lot of airsoft and paintball. They took large rucksacks and filled them with holsters, face masks, goggles, smaller bags, and some survival equipment. Dan thought Neil would be happy with a holster that wasn't on his thigh.

They took some webbing similar to their own, but not modern military-level stuff like theirs. The vague smell permeated everywhere, not strong, but they couldn't see any bodies yet. They found a large clothing shop, and Lexi managed a small grin, as it was the same chain she used to work for.

"Underwear and clothes for the kid?" she suggested to him. He nodded before moving into the store.

They retraced their steps to the Land Rover after a while longer to find two young men looking in the windows. The men hadn't noticed them yet, and Dan waved Lexi off to the right to get another angle on them.

Dan raised his carbine and stalked forward along the building line. He glanced to the right to see Lexi behind a pillar on one knee, covering the pair.

He watched them, listening.

"It wasn't here yesterday," said one of them.

"Well, where are they, then?" replied the other.

Dan guessed they were mid-twenties, and both looked fairly fit.

"Stand still," Dan called out confidently, without investing the command with much threat so as not to scare them.

In spite of his slightly gentler tone, both men visibly jumped in fright and turned towards the sound of his voice. They put their hands up and both started to speak at once.

"Hold on!" shouted Dan, but kindly. He lowered his weapon and walked towards them slowly, knowing that Lexi would have him covered and being careful not to get between her and them.

"I'm Mark," said the first man. He pointed to the slightly bigger man and introduced him as Joe.

"Put your hands down, boys. I'm not going to shoot you," Dan said, leaving out the fact that Lexi would if the need arose. "What's your story?" he asked Mark.

Both seemed frozen to the spot still. Joe managed a shop up the road, a Cash Converters place, and said that they had heard their car earlier. It turned out they had argued about whether to go out of the shop for a while, before deciding to introduce themselves.

Dan was going to unlock the Land Rover, until he realised that it was Lexi's and she still had the keys.

He turned towards her and gestured with his head for her to join them. Both Mark and Joe seemed shocked to see another heavily armed person appear.

Joe asked, "Are you from the military?"

Mark said, "Is there still a government?"

"No, and we don't know," said Dan. He introduced himself, then Lexi.

He asked what they had been doing for the last week and Joe told their story.

"Me and Mark have been in my shop, living off stuff we've found here," he said. Both looked unwashed and bearded, and it seemed they were both waiting for someone to come and tell them what to do. Neither seemed to accept that this was permanent.

Dan responded with a brief version of their own history, and explained their new setup. Both Mark and Joe seemed impressed and relieved. The formal invite came from Lexi, who had adopted a confident approach as she saw her own standing rising higher as more people joined.

Joe couldn't keep his eyes off their equipment, and finally asked, "M16s?"

"M4s. Long story," said Dan. "You have any experience?" he asked.

"Tried and failed. Asthma as a kid. Done some shooting – paintball and stuff," he said.

Dan chalked up another potential Ranger to take the pressure off.

"What about you?" he asked Mark.

"Never. I'm a PE teacher in high school. I was, anyway," he replied.

"Jump in then, lads; you're in if you want," said Dan as he climbed into the passenger's seat, wound down the window, and lit a smoke.

They drove back and dropped the two new arrivals off, where Penny greeted them warmly and took them in for feeding and washing. Dan said he was heading back out again, and told Lexi she should do the same on her own. She looked disappointed not to be staying with him, but agreed.

Dan decided to push out into the more rural areas from the prison, checking the farms for equipment and people.

He decided to leave messages at some, hidden away from the road, hopeful to recruit some farmers to their cause. As he rested for a short time having a smoke, he heard barking. He walked across the road to look downhill. The noise was coming from the bottom corner of the hill where the field met a dense patch of woodland. He opened the gate to the empty field and walked back to the Land Rover. He drove slowly down the hill with the windows opened. He killed the engine and listened when he reached the bottom. Definitely dogs barking on the other side of the woods. He looked at the map for a way to drive around, not just out of laziness but being sensible – why climb through woodland and risk injury or getting stuck?

He found a small track after a while on the Ordnance Survey map, realising that the way to it was actually past the prison on the road towards the town he had just been to.

Ten minutes later, he was driving down that track, over the bridge where the water from their lake went, and onwards to a house and a series of low buildings. A sign announced that he was entering a kennel, and he should take care, as police dogs were trained there. *Interesting.*

He pulled up by the house and got out. He left the carbine and took only his Sig as he walked around. A look through the window into the kitchen showed a man slumped on the table, dead over a week.

He heard the barking again, sounding louder now. He walked over to the outbuildings and what he saw made him feel sick with grief. Eight dogs had died in their kennels, with nobody to give them water. The stink of shit and piss was choking, and flies swarmed on the bodies. He walked along the line of closed cages close to tears, until he saw that the second to last in the line was empty. The wooden frame of this kennel had been chewed, destroyed in fact, and left a gap big enough for something to escape. He heard the barking again from outside.

He walked out and what he saw made his heart melt. A large, dusty grey German shepherd puppy was sitting between him and his vehicle with huge paws splayed out. It saw him and cocked its head to one side with its disproportionately large, pointy ears up. Dan went to bend down and pat its legs, but the puppy responded instantly by standing and barking aggressively at him. Puppy or not, there were a lot of sharp teeth on show. It was almost grey, with patches of darker fur on its ears, muzzle, and one paw. This dog looked thin and probably hadn't eaten for days. At least it hadn't died a torturous death by dehydration like the others. He froze, and the dog stopped again. He spoke to it, and the barking started.

Dan turned and went back into the kennels, coming back out with a sturdy leather lead. When he produced this, the puppy sat and looked at him, wagging its tail in the dirt. Part-trained, then. *Good.*

"Come," he said firmly, and was rewarded with another cocked-head look. An outside thought occurred to him, and he tried "*Hier!*" To his amazement, it worked, and the puppy trotted towards him. He had heard that some police forces had paid for part-trained dogs to be imported from Germany recently.

"Sitz!" he said, and the dog sat.

Dan hadn't spoken any German for a long time, and hoped nobody would question his knowledge of the language or of police dogs.

"Fuß!" he said, and he walked towards the Land Rover. The dog obediently walked to his left heel as he went. He laughed aloud and bent to stroke the dog, happy at this turn of fate. He snapped his hand back as the dog leapt away from him and became defensive again. He straightened up, shouting, "Nein. Halt!" Dan laughed again as the dog reluctantly stopped.

No matter how you felt, conditioning always took over. He tried some more.

"Shtopp!" he said, meaning stay, and he walked around the dog in a circle before walking away a few metres.

"Fuß!" he tried again, and the dog ran to his left side and followed him at heel. He had exhausted his current memory of German, and carefully went to put the lead around the dog's neck. A low growl came out, but a further reprimand stopped the noise in its throat.

He led the dog to the Land Rover and was lost for a command. "Hup!" he said, and the dog jumped in. "Shtopp!" he instructed again, leaving the lead on and the door open. He went back and took two large metal bowls and a bag of dried dog food which he slung over his shoulder. He threw them in the boot and walked to the passenger's side, where the dog sat, watching him.

He slowly raised the back of his hand. The dog sniffed it suspiciously, eyes wary. Dan saw that it was a he, and saw that he had no collar. With the beautiful colouring, he decided that his new best friend was called Ash.

SETTLING IN NICELY

He drove back to the prison and stopped on the farm. Ana waved at him, carrying a bucket of leftover food to the pigs.

He left Ash in the Land Rover, as he didn't want to risk him biting anyone or chasing any of the animals. He wandered into the new workshop and saw Neil and Ian had been busy – a generator was set up to provide power, and the spare wheels, complete with inflated tyres for the Defenders, were stacked against one wall.

"Cooking on gas, my son!" Neil announced in a cockney accent when he saw him. Ian looked up and nodded a greeting.

"Met the new recruits?" Dan asked them, and described finding Mark and Joe earlier.

"How's Lexi?" Neil asked with a smirk. Dan refused to rise to the bait. It wasn't just him who had noticed it, then.

Dan changed the subject. "I've got a new assistant," he said, gesturing Neil to follow him outside.

Neil's heart melted, and he let out a large "Awww" when he saw Ash looking out of the driver's window at him.

"He's no pet. I found him in a kennels where they trained police dogs," Dan warned.

Neil said that he used to have a retired police dog, and had no problem with it.

Dan opened the door of the Defender and took hold of Ash's lead. "Fuß!" he said, and Ash jumped down to walk at his left heel. He walked to Neil, stopping short and saying, "Sitz!"

He looked at Neil and asked, "Sprechen Sie Deutsch?" with a smile.

Neil didn't, but he did launch into an impression of a German officer as he extolled the virtues of the dog. He went to stroke him at one point, and was rewarded with an angry salvo of barks.

"Nein," shouted Dan, and Ash calmed down. "Give him time, mate. He's had a rough week, I think."

They said their goodbyes, and Dan drove back down to the main house. He saw that some wooden pallets had been laid on the floor, three across and two deep, with tarpaulins fixed to the back. Jay had started felling a tree to the side of the main drive, wearing a hard hat with ropes coiled like snakes. He waved cheerily to Dan when he saw he was being watched. Liam was standing some distance back, seemingly on instruction, waiting for the tree to come down. He was holding a heavy set of long-handled loppers and a bow saw, ready to start taking branches off. That tree would take them a few days to sort, thought Dan.

He took Ash in through the front door, greeting Leah as he walked in. She cried, "You got a puppy!" and ran towards him just as Ash strained at the lead and barked at her. She shrieked and stopped in her tracks. Dan repeated the advice he had given Neil – that Ash had been through a lot and wasn't exactly a pet; he had been bred to bite people.

He took Ash into his room and folded two prison blankets in the corner of the room by his cot. He went back outside and brought in the bowls and food, laying them down as Ash started to sniff them desperately. He wolfed down a bowl of food and stopped only to switch to the bowl Dan was pouring water into from a bottle.

He left him there and went outside, shutting him in. He spent a few minutes with Leah, who had been busy making pretty lists covered in highlighter marks in pink and yellow and blue. She had lined up weeks' worth of scavenging targets. Dan told her she had done a good job, and to take the afternoon off to play, as it was nice outside. She skipped off, happy with the praise.

He stored his carbine and poured a cup of coffee from the dining room – Penny had found some large insulated pump flasks which held boiling water and kept it hot for hours. He wandered into the medical wing to see Mike sitting up in his makeshift hospital bed with his nose buried in the book about solar panels.

A notepad covered with scribbled notes was by his right leg, and he tapped the pen against his teeth as he read. He smiled when he saw Dan and launched into a complex explanation of how he hoped to use the solar panels but ideally needed some scaffolding. Dan held up his hands to slow him down, as he didn't understand most of what he was saying.

"Plenty of time, Mike. Get your head around it and get better first," he said.

He found Mark and Joe being given a tour by Penny. Both had washed and dressed in new clothes: combat trousers and T-shirts over walking boots. Mark had shaved, but Joe hadn't. Dan rubbed his own chin and thought about growing a beard to avoid having to shave with cold water.

Penny greeted him warmly but formally in front of the new arrivals, congratulating him for bringing back two healthy recruits. Eve looked unhappy as she carried an armful of dirty clothes to a large wheeled cart, the young girl clinging to her trouser leg.

Jimmy and Kev had come back not long after him; they were unloading their latest shop with the help of Andrew, who was directing them where he wanted things.

He went back to his room and could hear loud whining from Ash inside. Suddenly remembering that the puppy had barely eaten or drunk for days, he thought he better take him outside on the lead. Ash made for the nearest car tyre and relieved himself before sniffing the ground and spinning on the spot. He finally decided to leave a steaming log at the first place he had sniffed before bouncing away, pleased with himself. Dan walked him down to the nearest sports field.

He made the dog sit, removed his lead, and walked away, telling Ash to stay. He decided to give commands in both English and German, to save having to be bilingual. He stopped and looked at Ash before throwing his arm out to the side and calling, "Go!" Ash hesitated.

"Voraus!" he said, and the dog bolted off to the right, looking for the reason he had been sent. He sniffed the ground and then looked up at Dan, who called him back in. "Fuß! Heel," he said, and smiled when Ash ran to his left side, looking up at him.

Eat your heart out, Pete, he thought. In truth, he knew it was cheating. Someone else had already done the hard work in training this dog; he was looking good and reaping the benefits of it.

Pete returned a while later on foot with the dogs flitting around him. He was carrying two rabbits and five pigeons. He saw Dan's new sidekick and told his girls to stay as he approached. He held up his haul with a big smile.

"Plenty of vermin to eat," he said happily. "These woods are full of pheasants too, but they're breeding, so I'll leave them be until the numbers get high. No worry about these buggers, though," he said, indicating his haul.

Dan thanked him, wishing that a rabbit-and-pigeon stew would be accompanied by fresh bread. Pete nodded to Ash, who gave him a look as though he was figuring out if he were edible.

"Found him at a kennels. He'd escaped, but the others starved. Part-trained police dog," Dan said, trying to sound casual despite his pride at having Ash beside him.

"Good dog," Pete said, holding his hand out. Ash didn't bark, which surprised Dan. Instead, he sniffed at Pete's hands, getting a mixture of dead animals and other dogs. *He must recognise a fellow dog lover*, Dan thought.

Word of Ash had spread quickly, and people made noises fit for a puppy until they saw that the puppy had a genetically created bad attitude and sharp teeth. Dan put Ash back in his room so as not to excite him too much.

Cedric and Maggie returned not long after, excited at having found a commercial garden area with greenhouses and polythene tunnels. It seemed to be part of the prison, but was about a mile away and had more tractors, machinery, and all the tools they needed. They said there was even a house there that they could look to move into if they needed. There were even two dozen sheep there – this year's lambs, Cedric reckoned – and a large animal trailer.

They had brought back another Land Rover they had found, towing a trailer of rotting veg, which they dropped off at the farm for the pigs. They spoke excitedly to Penny, saying that they could grow potatoes and carrots there as well as salad vegetables. Penny agreed for them to be there full time, and promised them a helping pair of hands or five as soon as they were found.

A huge sound erupted as they were talking, taking everyone by surprise. Dan instinctively reached for the Sig but relaxed when he saw that it was the large tree finally giving up and coming down to the ground.

The house buzzed with the excitement of the day's news and new arrivals when Lexi returned last. He watched her drive towards the house, and saw at least two other heads in the Defender with her. She pulled up at the front and got out, looking proud but trying to keep it under control.

"Boss," she said, "meet Lizzie." As a woman climbed out of the passenger's seat, she smiled nervously at him. "And this is Cara," said Lexi as she opened the rear doors. "And Josh."

Dan saw that Cara was young – maybe twenty – and he placed Josh at about three. He was a good-looking boy with blue eyes and bright blonde hair. Dan stifled a choked cry; he looked too much like his own son for him to cope just now.

He mumbled a welcome and excused himself, letting Penny take over and welcome them in. He stripped off his boots and got into the grey tracksuit again, then lay on his cot. Ash watched him closely, making him feel slightly uncomfortable after a while. Dan held out his hand to the dog, who recoiled at first, then sniffed and licked at his hand. Ash finally lay down with Dan's hand resting on the back of his head, and slept.

He always envied dogs that ability. Two speeds: flat out and spark out.

He took Ash out again about an hour later, walking him at heel while he led, and then he shut Ash away again before dinner. The mood was high throughout the meal, and Penny had invited the new arrivals to say a bit about themselves.

Lizzie was a nursing assistant who worked for a care company. She spent her days visiting people at home and helping them, changing dressings and the like. As she said this, Kate said loudly, "Mine!" and everyone laughed.

Cara was in college, having had Josh in her late teens to an absent boyfriend. Dan imagined that some people would have had an opinion on that two weeks ago, but those kinds of grievances were void now. Josh was quiet and nervous, understandably.

Penny called for departmental heads to stay while the others went to the lounge area. Penny made a short speech about how happy she was with the way the group was holding together and growing.

"I hear talk of another new addition to the group?" she said proudly.

"Absolutely!" said Dan with a smile, referring to Ash. His mood was improving now he had got used to the presence of Josh enough to see that he bore less and less of a resemblance to his own son every time he looked at him.

"Lizzie has obviously been taken by medical – no arguments there, I think," she said. Kate looked relieved to have some backup.

"Cara has expressed experience in catering. I propose to have her cooking for now, with Eve attached for training. The children should be fine with them. All agreed?" All did agree, and Penny's obvious look of relief made it clear just how stressed she was at producing meals on top of organising.

"Joe has asked to join the Rangers," she said, looking at Dan. That was no surprise; he seemed a bit of an army nut.

"Pending assessment, yes," said Dan, and he reminded them that he had the final say on whether someone got a gun or not. He saw an eagerness in Joe that appeared not to be bolstered by arrogance and felt happy to be patient with him. The skills could be taught, but the temperament needed to be the solid foundation for teaching.

"Mark has offered his services wherever they may be required, as he has no children to teach sports to," she finished.

Jimmy straightened in his seat. "I'll take him," he said eagerly.

"Logistics it is, then," she declared.

DEVELOPMENTS

The next month moved on quickly for them.

Dan spent time each morning for the first five days working with Ash, making sure he was OK around the others and getting obedient. He made sure Ash was fine with Joe, as Dan spent that first week teaching him weapon drills, building searches, maintenance, and target practice. Dan had kitted him out with Neil's Glock and leg holster, as they were custom-made for the weapons, and the scavenged webbing was fitted to him. They used the gym for the building drills, making Joe drive up and search, with Dan observing and pointing out where he made mistakes. He resisted the urge to yell "Bang!" every time he left himself open.

He had given Joe a standard M4 with a reflex sight, as he wasn't that accurate through a scope. Dan worked with him until he was over-average accurate at forty metres. Good enough. The first time he'd got him to shoot, Dan had left the gun empty deliberately. As he had expected, Joe flinched when he pulled the trigger. They worked to eradicate that instinct, and moved on to live rounds. He couldn't afford to expend too much ammo in training without getting more stockpiled.

As they worked, Ash sat some distance back, where he had been told to stay, and watched them. Ash was getting bigger every day and responded to English commands now, but Dan still used German sometimes to show off.

Joe was OK behind the wheel, and had even done a day off-roading recently with a Land Rover instructor. Dan showed him how to use the front and rear tow ropes, too.

Jay and Liam were making good progress with the tree, and Dan reckoned they already had a few tons of logs ready for winter. They would have to triple that before the weather got any worse, and it was already getting colder. A few storms had made them all take cover inside for hours at a time. They started to plan scavenging for the onset of bad weather, getting hot-water bottles and cold-weather gear.

Mark had taken a shine to Lexi, which thankfully kept her away from Dan a bit. Neil and Ian had retrieved three more Defenders, two of which went into a shed on the farm until they were needed and the other was presented to Joe when he was officially declared a Ranger, albeit on probation.

Cara had been a godsend in the kitchen, and was the one person Eve didn't complain to. She was skilled at making cakes, and also baked some bread and made pastry for game pies, as Pete had been bringing back a steady supply of rabbits and pigeons daily. Cara was named acting Head of Catering, as she was reluctant to take on a leadership role, and agreed to stay in that post until someone better was found. She was just happy to cook and be with the kids, the former making her popular overnight.

Pete maintained that there were plenty of other things to hunt, but he knew about the breeding seasons and wanted the populations to stay healthy. He had been allocated a workshop as such over on "the gardens," as they were now being called, which had previously been a butcher's area. Good-quality knives were found, and the old gamekeeper settled into a routine of getting out after breakfast to check the snares he had left the night before. There was no sign of his drinking being an issue, although Dan did find a couple of bottles stashed in his butcher's shop.

Cedric and Maggie were the happiest of all. They left every day for the gardens to clear the greenhouses and polytunnels, ready to plant some vegetables after Christmas. Maggie had studied a book from the library in depth and knew what they had to do each month.

As he expected, Leah had grown bored after the initial phase of planning everything, and Dan decided to give her something new to learn. Neil had started teaching the members of the group who were either too young or unqualified to drive. Liam did well, and Ana was picking it up slowly. Kyle and Leah struggled, Leah because she was young and Kyle because he was lazy. Jimmy kept Kyle in check, and Dan worried that he was working him too hard at times.

Jimmy and Kev still made scavenging trips, but as the stores were almost full, it wasn't the top priority. They helped out on the farm and the gardens, then spent a few hours hauling logs before dinner. Everyone got into a good routine, and the general mood was one of happiness and hope.

Mike was moving around well but still tired quickly. Every day he built his strength up a little more by walking the grounds, often joining Dan as he worked Ash. He declared the solar panel project viable, but needed scaffolding and skilled people like builders. Dan agreed it should go on hold until next summer. In the meantime, Mike was working on rainwater collection and had already asked Jimmy and Kev to get a lorryload of materials ready for when he was fitter.

They had a new addition after a few days; a young man from one of the farms Dan had visited found his message and had come calling on a quad bike. He was called Chris, and he was excited at the prospect of joining. He knew about maintaining livestock, which made him a valuable person to the cause. He had left that morning with a promise to return, and came back hours later on the quad bike herding some sheep. He made numerous return trips over the next few days, bringing other animals using the cattle box from the gardens. He took over on the farm and moved animals around. Nobody argued with him, as nobody had the knowledge. He was a hard-working man, thin as a rake and ginger – so much so that he joked about getting sunburn whenever the cloud cover broke – but he had a seemingly endless supply of energy and enjoyed life every day.

He was named Head of Agriculture and given a seat on "the council," as Penny called it. She had offered Cedric and Maggie a place also, but they declined politely. They were just happy to be together and garden all day. Dan suspected that they would want to move over there eventually, but he worried that they were exposed enough as it was. He didn't have the spare bodies to post a guard, and said as much to Andrew, who suggested an alarm system.

"How about a big box of fireworks?" Andrew said during a meeting. "Light fuse and hide until help comes!"

Dan had to admit that was actually a pretty good plan in the absence of any real-time communications. Jimmy and Kev were dispatched and did a fine job of bringing back an all-in-one box: Light fuse and stand clear as forty small rockets shot up one by one. Cedric set it up on a raised platform with a solid cover over the top; all they had to do was remove the cover and light the paper.

At the end of the first week, Lexi brought back another two people. Donna was mid-thirties and had been out of work for a while. She was assigned to Penny to help with cleaning and did not complain. Matt, or "Matty," as he preferred, was still overweight somehow. It seemed that he had survived on chocolate bars and fizzy drinks for two months (and probably longer before), and he was assigned to help Cedric and Maggie on the gardens. He was happy with this, and happier still to be fed every day.

Lexi was ranging every other day, and on the second week, Joe was sent on a few missions close to home. Dan had spent time with both of them, drumming into their heads what to do if they were attacked or compromised. What to do with a vehicle failure. What to do if they were lost. What to do if they had to abandon their vehicles and start escape and evade, or E&E protocols. He checked their kit at random intervals, inspecting weapon readiness and cleanliness and emptying their rucksacks out to see that they had everything they needed if they had to go on the run.

He started to go out on his own again, working with Ash to use him as backup on building searches and developing a deep bond with the dog. He reasoned that Ash was a tool that increased his effectiveness, but he knew that the dog kept him company. It was someone he could talk to, as he did often, but who wouldn't tell his secrets or judge. Ash listened intently, with both ears up facing him and his head cocked over slightly.

Dan was planning to find another source of weapons and ammo, as the 5.56 stocks were almost a quarter gone. He decided, without telling the others, that he was going to head south again. He avoided Leah, who would ask people leaving home where they were going to be, and told the council that he may be away overnight.

He set off after breakfast with his E&E bag containing the right maps and an extra bag of kit with food and water for him and Ash.

Ash seemed excited, as though he sensed they were going somewhere new this time.

Clouds gathered as he left home, giving a sense of foreboding.

RETURN TRIP

He went slowly, cautiously retracing their steps of over a month ago. Nothing much seemed to have changed, Dan thought as he wound past their former camp. The gazebo had collapsed, one loose side flapping against the abandoned caravan. Either nobody had found the place, or nobody had stayed.

Some people would deem his planned course of action reckless, but he considered the chance of finding "them" at the same place he did previously slim. He drove gently, not forcing the engine note much higher than tickover, and parked the Land Rover under a tree off the road. A new vehicle dumped on the tarmac would set his alarm bells going, and he hoped his small deception would keep them safe.

He got out and readied his weapon, checking chamber and flicking the safety catch to full auto then back to safe. Ash bounded out with him, happy to be back on the ground. He ran in two small circles of the Land Rover before cocking his leg against the back wheel. Dan fixed him with a stern look and held his flat palm out towards the dog before slowly moving it down.

Ash got the message; his tail stopped wagging and he lowered himself into a stalking crouch. Dan turned the gesture into a quiet pat on his thigh and Ash loped to his left heel. Dan had worked hard on this, and it paid off. He could work Ash with hand signals most of the time, unless he got bored or overexcited. He was trying to stop Ash barking too, but needed a live subject to help with that. He didn't want to set Ash on any of the group in case Ash didn't realise it was training.

They went slowly, moving between cover to minimise the risk of exposure before they came to the place where he and Lexi had saved Mike and Alice. Everything was just as he had left it, apart from the decomposing bodies and small rivers of maggots coming from both dead men. The new addition to his kit was useful then; a black bandana knotted around his neck was pulled up to cover his mouth and nose.

Ash went forward to sniff, and a click of Dan's fingers brought him back obediently. He decided that the friends of these two arseholes either never found them or just left them there to rot. Either was highly likely.

Hanging around to explore wasn't the point of this trip, and he still had some distance to cover. They got back in the Land Rover, Dan still not entirely convinced they were safe from those they had run to hide from. He again followed the road he had been down many times before, trying to recall the journey to see if anything had changed – another car abandoned, a sign or a message, anything.

He had decided, despite the veiled warning, to check the army base again. Just a drive past, nothing too intrusive. As he went by, he saw the gates were open. He turned around and came past again – still no sign of life. "Fuck it," he said to himself, receiving a silent questioning look from Ash, and drove in.

Nobody showed themselves. More importantly, he felt, nobody took a shot at him. He drove slowly between the buildings, finding the doors left wide open to many. He began to suspect that the occupant he had met previously was no longer here. He found the armoury by chance, not because it was marked "armoury," but because he went inside to investigate the pair of boots attached to the pair of legs he could see from the doorway.

He had only seen a thing like this once before. A shotgun would make a horrendous mess of a person at short range. At point-blank range, and using heavy ammunition, it would literally dismember.

The soldier – he assumed the same one he had met before, but could not tell, as there was no head – must have had enough. He was sitting with an empty bottle of gin next to him, slumped against the wall, which had been sprayed with a grotesque fan of blood, brains, and bone. The wall was deeply gouged by shot. Flies were thick on the man, and Dan thought twice about disturbing his final resting place save for retrieving the shotgun; it was a chunky short-barrelled one with a folding parachute stock that went over the top of it. That was just too valuable to leave behind. A note was in his left hand but had fallen into the congealed puddle of blood. Dan was grateful that he wasn't able to read the note as he felt compelled to do; the contents would likely be more upsetting than the gore in front of him. Dan apologised sincerely to the now headless soldier as he took his sidearm and spare ammunition. He stripped the body armour, similar to his own but in green camouflage. It badly needed a wash. He found some plastic wrapping and bundled everything he had taken off the man together. The shotgun wasn't too bad, so it went on the dash of the Land Rover.

With a shudder, he turned away and tried to focus: *Find more ammo.* He searched boxes and shelves as Ash walked patiently beside him. Finally, he struck lucky in one of the now unlocked secure rooms. He took thousands of rounds of 5.56 – box after box. He took another three boxes of link ammo for the GPMG; it would be a bad day if they ever had to use that, but still. He found more 9mm and took as much as he could load into the rear of the Land Rover, so much so that the rear-view mirror was useless. A box of heavy twelve-bore cartridges was left out from when the soldier had decided on his exit strategy.

Dan reminded himself to keep those separate from all the other shotgun ammo. If Pete hit a pigeon with one of these, he would atomise it.

He considered staying for more, but thought that greed might blind him to the risks; this was not a place to hang around in. He took one last look around the lockers but could find no more weapons, only more locked doors. This place would no doubt be a gold mine; he knew there were military vehicles here as well as lots of guns. He was, however, way too strung out and nervous to stay any longer. He had a bad feeling about this place and wanted to get out of there.

Dan opened the door of the Land Rover, telling Ash "Hup" softly. A quick scan around showed no overt sign of people, but the feeling was still there. As if to underline his point, Ash began to growl quietly and look around. He was nervous too.

He drove hard at first, struggling, as the vehicle was weighed down, then stopped away from the road and waited with his carbine pointed towards the direction his fear was coming from. He drove on, repeating this twice more before he relaxed enough to convince himself that they were not being followed. His alertness had tired him greatly, and Ash had already given up and lain down on the seat, annoyed that the comfortable part of the car was full of boxes. He stopped at the forecourt where he had stayed after his last trip to the area, where he had marvelled at his new toys. He poured himself a coffee and lit up – Ash grumbled and growled if he smoked in the car with him.

In a way, it was nice to be nagged from the passenger's seat again.

He caught his reflection in the glass of the shop window. He needed to sort his hair out, he thought as his wild homeless-looking image stared back at him. Ash trotted around the forecourt sniffing at things before coming to sit in front of Dan. He pulled off his signature move: ears up, pointy tips almost meeting in the middle and head cocked to one side.

Damn this dog, thought Dan as he reached into his bag for a snack to share with him. Ash was growing so fast and eating so much that an extra item was added to the scavenging list: big bags of dog food. His paws were still ridiculously oversized, making Dan think that this puppy was going to be a small bear before long.

Ash suddenly turned his head away and stopped chewing, alert and tense. Dan froze, waiting to find out what the dog's far superior hearing had detected. A low growl rumbled from Ash's chest as he got to his feet, staring intently in the direction they had come from.

That was enough for Dan. He threw down the cigarette and tipped the coffee, throwing all his things back into the Land Rover via the open window. He readied his weapon and double-checked the Sig. As he took position behind the bonnet of his vehicle, he called Ash's name and was rewarded by instant eye contact. He threw his left arm out and shouted, "GO" as Ash launched himself low and fast across the forecourt to hide in the shadows. To make sure Ash knew what he wanted of him, he followed up with, "Down! Stay!"

The dog obediently lay down flat and watched him intently. He was confident that Ash would stay there until either he called him to heel or shouted a go command, at which point he hoped Ash would attack whatever he was looking at. He also hoped that the dog would take the initiative if he was incapacitated and protect him.

The diesel engine came into Dan's hearing, followed a short time later by a muddy 4x4 coming towards him at speed. The engine note halted, like the driver had lifted off the throttle at the surprise of seeing his Land Rover. There seemed to be some hesitation, then a decision as the driver turned in sharply to stop alongside Dan's vehicle.

A vaguely familiar blonde ponytail was showing behind the mud-spattered window. Although the 4x4 was different from the one he last saw her with, the woman was unmistakably the same frosty vet.

She was momentarily speechless at recognising him, but gathered herself.

"I'm being chased!" she said, annoyed. "I caught the bastards shooting horses to eat!"

Great, he thought, *some hungry Frenchmen are heading this way.* He snapped into gear.

"How many?" he demanded, loosening the Velcro strap on the pouch where two spare magazines sat snugly.

"Three. No, four," she blurted out.

"Still got your shotgun?" he asked her as he scanned through his optic at the limit of his view on the road.

"No. They took it. I, er, I bit the one holding me and stole one of their cars," she said, almost embarrassed.

"OK," said Dan, "so we're not *negotiating* with them, then?" he asked with heavy emphasis to make his point understood.

"No, we are bloody well not. They shot my horses. They would probably have eaten me too, fucking inbred bastards," she spat angrily.

"Open the passenger door, and look on the dash," he told her, still looking through his scope.

She did as he said and retrieved the new shotgun. She looked at it uncertainly.

"Pump-action. Hell of a kick, so hold it tight, OK?"

Sera nodded, which Dan couldn't see. He was thinking of where to send her so that she was a tactical advantage but wouldn't shoot him or Ash by accident. He brought up a picture of the area they were occupying in his mind, and came up with a plan. He could hear engines in the distance, so had probably a few seconds to make clear what he wanted.

"Stand here. Let them see you. Get them in close to talk," he said as he vacated his position for her.

She raised the gun as he moved backwards, reaching back past her to flick the safety catch on the shotgun she held.

"And don't, for fuck's sake, shoot my dog!" he called as he ran behind the vehicles to hide across the road.

Sera was scared and confused. More confused than scared, in truth; she couldn't see a dog and was worrying that the man – she couldn't remember his name – was possibly insane. Frying pan, fire?

Her wandering mind was brought to heel when a pickup truck sped into view. She tightened her grip on the curiously sticky shotgun and wondered where the crazy man and his imaginary dog had gone.

WE DO NOT NEGOTIATE

Dan heard then saw the green twin-cab Hilux scream over the crest of the road. He had positioned himself opposite his Land Rover, with a field of fire that hopefully wouldn't hit Sera or Ash.

As he expected, the idiots drove straight for her without the first sense of self-preservation. He prayed they didn't disappoint him by being clever. Four men piled out of the truck, angry. One was holding his right hand with a rag pressed to it. Two others had firearms: long guns. The last was empty-handed.

"That's far enough," yelled Sera.

Jesus, thought Dan, *this is getting far too like a Wild West film to be true.*

"What's the matter, girlie?" asked one of the men holding a gun in a very thick country accent.

No longer caring at all if he were accused of stereotyping someone, Dan decided that this serial underachiever had probably spent his formative years sexually abusing a sibling. As this was the one to speak first, Dan very much doubted that any of them were the clever one of the group.

"Go away or you will regret it!" she shouted.

The idiots laughed among themselves. Typical bullies.

Dan started to move his optic slowly from left to right, between the heads of the two holding guns. Running through the practices in his head, he was sure he could drop both primary threats within a couple of seconds.

"You sick fucking bastards!" Sera yelled at them. "Killing horses? What's wrong with you?" She was angry.

Perfect, thought Dan, *keep their attention on you.*

"Put that down and come with us; you'll see we can be nice," idiot number one said, prompting sick chuckles from idiots two to four inclusively. That was enough for Dan. He had a disagreement on principle with rapists.

Flicking the safety catch to semi-automatic, he dropped idiot one with a shot to the head. It wasn't difficult from that range, as the oblivious victim's face took up most of the scope. He swung the optic onto where idiot two was still standing in perfect profile to him, frozen in shock. Dan shot him just under the left ear, killing him instantly as his brainstem fountained from the ruined base of his skull.

He rose from his hiding place like a predator emerging from cover and advanced towards the remaining two idiots, neither of which had yet figured out what had happened. Idiot three finally woke up and made completely the wrong choice. Bellowing like a branded bull, he dived forward to get the shotgun from the lifeless hands of idiot one. Dan flicked the selector to automatic and fired two bursts. All of the rounds hit the man in the chest, who fell to the ground like a ragdoll rasping his last few bubbling breaths.

Idiot four was still holding his badly bitten hand, and now had idiot two's blood splattered on the right side of his face.

Dan lowered the M4 and slung it on his back.

Sera marched forward, livid. "This doesn't work!" she shouted, waving the stubby shotgun at Dan.

"That's because I put the safety on. I told you I didn't want you shooting my dog," he replied.

"What dog? You're insane!" she shouted.

Idiot four thought this was the perfect time to make his escape, and he ran. Dan and Sera stopped arguing to watch the ridiculous sight of a man sprinting in panic, the fear scrambling his ability to coordinate limb movement.

Dan turned to face her and smiled. "Voraus!" he shouted, and a streak of grey and black bolted from behind her, bringing down the running man in a swirl of snarls and screams of pain.

It seemed that the vet was very touchy about animals dying. She was less concerned with people, as she made clear to idiot four before she dispatched him using Dan's Sig, which he had offered her in exchange for the brutal shotgun. It was a kindness in a way; Ash had proven himself quite the hunter when given the chance.

"Don't think I'm like that all the time," she told him, still quite aggressive in her tone. "That piece of shit was going to rape me, and God knows how many others." He guessed this was her form of guilt at taking a life: the aggressive justification coping method.

"No argument from me," he said as he dragged the last of the four bodies off the road. "What now?" he asked, collecting the guns and ammunition.

Sera didn't know. Dan suggested that she come back with him, but she immediately started to list excuses. He held up a hand but she continued to rant, even breaking out into a change of octave.

He had heard enough, and the now waning dose of adrenaline made him snap more harshly than he intended. "SHUT UP!" he said in his most commanding voice. "Christ, you would give a deaf man a headache! No wonder you spend your life with animals!"

That shut her up briefly. Before she launched into another tirade, he cut her off. "You aren't safe on your own. The end. We have farm animals that need tending to. You can be useful to us and be safe. You are coming back."

"Well, I'm not going in your car with that!" she said, pointing at Ash, and knowing that he was the subject of discussion, he cocked his head again and waited forlornly for praise.

"He's not dangerous," Dan yelled.

"Tell that to him!" she replied, pointing up the road to where Ash had brought down the man.

"You're the one who killed him!" he shouted back.

"THAT'S NOT THE POINT!" screamed Sera back at him as tears sparkled at the corners of her eyes.

He bit back his next line. They were obviously the kind of people who would argue over anything and everything. Plus, he recalled, there was little to gain from arguing with a woman under any circumstances.

"What then?" he asked, deliberately lowering his voice. "Stay here? Become a victim of people like that?" He gestured towards the bodies.

"I don't know!" she said, the first tears breaking through her prickly exterior.

"Then come with us," Dan said, pleading.

Sera thought for a minute, before holding up her hand and cuffing away her tears. "Please, will you help me get my things first?" she asked.

"Yes. Where and what? Because we need to move soon," he replied, relieved.

"Back where they found me," she said, and got back into her stolen vehicle.

A few minutes later, Dan drove into a small equestrian yard behind her. He saw two horses immobile on the ground in a paddock, and another was prancing around in fear.

She abandoned the stolen car and went to a small lorry marked "HORSES." She started the truck and began piling in boxes from her own car marked with the livery of the veterinary company. She caught the scared horse and led it into the back of the lorry up the noisy ramp before going to catch three more.

Dan had left Ash in the Land Rover, as he had that canine obsession of picking fights with animals ten times his size the second you took your eye off him. He scanned the area constantly through his scope, wary of another countryside relations meeting.

Sera announced she was nearly ready, but needed a hand with some hay bales. Dan lifted a few, but space was soon running out. He threw another eight on his roof rack and hastily tied them down with the ratchet straps he had used to secure the spare wheels.

He set off with Sera following in the lorry. Progress was slow, as she was careful of the four horses in the back as well as the storm of hay flying from Dan's roof load towards her windscreen.

The light started to fade as they were still at best an hour away from home, maybe two with their current rate of progress. He slowed and hit his hazard lights briefly to warn Sera that he was stopping. He rolled to a halt on a large, wide stretch of empty road.

He walked up to her window, lighting a cigarette. "Won't make it back before pitch-black; we can either go on slowly or plot up for the night somewhere." He gave her the choice. She couldn't decide, so he offered more reasoning. "It's slightly more dangerous moving at night now. For a start, there's no lighting, and we would be very easy to follow with the noise and the light we're putting out."

She told him that they should do whatever he thought, and he realised that all of her infuriating bluster had gone. Exhaustion and stress, probably.

He led on slowly, eventually finding a small field off the main road with a stable block. Sera let the horses out into the paddock. Dan let Ash out after they were shut away, but he still ran over to them for a closer look.

"Nein. Fuß!" he called, and the dog reluctantly trotted back to his side.

"Show-off," Sera muttered.

Dan fed Ash, boiled some water on a camp kettle, and broke out his rations. He realised Sera hadn't brought any clothes or a sleeping bag. He brought out his emergency bag, giving her a sleeping mat and bag. He heated tins of food in a pan and they shared the meal in silence, watched carefully by Ash, who was waiting for any leftovers.

He lay there fully clothed in his sleeping bag, Ash pressed lengthways alongside him for warmth and snoring happily. He could not sleep, so he quietly shifted and lit a cigarette.

As the flame briefly illuminated their shelter, Dan saw that Sera was awake too and looking straight at him. "Can't sleep?" he asked softly, not wanting to wake up Ash.

"No," she replied in almost a whisper. "Can I have one of those, please?" she asked.

He silently passed the lit cigarette to her and lit another. She made no complaint, accepting it in silence. The two lay there smoking, no words passing between them. He was sure that if they did speak, it would rapidly turn into an argument anyway, so he was happy she wasn't yelling at him.

She shifted position and stubbed the cigarette out on the timber wall behind her.

"Thank you," she said warmly. He was sure she meant for more than just the smoke.

EXPLAIN YOURSELF, MAN!

Dan led Sera to the gardens by late morning, where she put the horses into the stable block and unloaded the hay. In their haste to leave, she realised she had only brought head collars for them and no tack. Dan asked what "tack" was, inviting a patronising explanation that it meant saddles and bridles. Dan was about to bite back that they – the horsey types – should just say that instead of inventing another word to confuse the lower classes, but they were interrupted by Maggie and Cedric arriving in their new old Land Rover Defender and a smiling Matty sitting in the back.

Introductions were made, and Dan excused them, as they were very tired and needed to get back to the house. Sera let the horses out and Maggie promised to put them away before they came back for dinner. The horse transporter was left in situ and Sera had to accept a lift in Dan's Land Rover, much to her disgust, as Ash was made to stand on the boxes in the back and didn't take his eyes off her.

Penny was her usual effusive self as she greeted her newest duckling to the nest. She sat with them around the remnants of the breakfast spread and spoke as Dan and Sera ate. The story of how she had come to be with them had not yet come out, but his claim of having found thousands of rounds of ammo and the mention of Sera being a vet finally put the ducks in a row.

"Sera," she said coldly. "Would you kindly please give us the room?" It was an instruction not to be ignored, not a question indicating a choice of compliance.

Sera gave an amused look to Dan, probably relishing the fact that he was in trouble, and walked out, followed by Cara and the other couple of people left around. No doubt they would all hear what was to be said, but Penny was too polite to rip someone a new hole in front of others.

"Tell me," she began softly, "exactly where you have been, Daniel?"

He decided to get it all out in one go. "South. Into the area I declared was out of bounds. I checked the area where Lexi and I killed the two bikers, then our old camp. No sign that our presence was discovered or followed. I then went back to the army base and found the soldier dead."

"You stupid, reckless man!" Penny interjected, unable to contain her indignation any longer. "We rely on you for our safety and you go and break your own rules made expressly to keep us all safe? You said yourself that this soldier had skills far superior to your own – who is so dangerous that they could have killed him? Do you not understand the danger you put yourself and all of us in?" By this point, she was almost turning purple with the effort of keeping her voice below a shout.

Dan cut in. "He blew his own damned head off, Penny. Literally. No head. Gone. Ever seen what that's like? Would you like me to describe it in detail?" he asked nastily. Penny never did cope well with the gory details. She didn't start in again, so he continued, "I then managed to get more guns and ammunition, enough to last a hell of a lot longer than we could have. Then I saved a vet from being raped and brought back a very useful person and four horses."

"How exactly did you save her?" Penny asked warily, expecting the answer that he had killed someone.

"I shot the two with guns in the head. Another one tried to shoot me so I shot him first. The last one tried to run away, but seeing as I'm no longer bound to catching rapists only for them to get away with it, Ash chased him down and Sera killed him," he finished angrily, breathing hard as his voice rose with each line he spoke.

A curious look fell over Penny, like she had just learned something valuable, and was gone as soon as he saw it.

"And besides," he said more gently, "I never said it was out of bounds for me."

"You deliberately deceived us," Penny answered. "You failed to follow your own protocols and leave your route and itinerary with Leah; believe me, I checked, and the girl tried to cover it up for you!" That seemed to annoy her the most.

He was secretly very impressed that Leah had tried to have his back. He must make that up to her.

"Penny," Dan said quietly. He was tired. He needed to carry a lot of boxes of brass and clean four weapons – two of which had congealed brains on them – before he could settle down to rest. "It worked out OK in the end," he held up a hand to stop her furious objection at that, "but I apologise for not telling you where I was going. I won't do that again, but you must trust me to make my own decisions when it comes to these things."

Penny was silent, waiting for more.

"It was dangerous, which is why I went and did not send any of the others," he finished.

"Not good enough," she said.

"Well, if you don't mind, I have lots to do, and I haven't slept in two days," he snapped as he stood and walked out.

A flurry of footsteps scattered from the door before he opened it, only to find lots of innocent people minding their own business nearby. He didn't care. He walked back to his room, woke up Ash, who was already asleep on his cot, and went outside. He lit a smoke and started to pile boxes out of the Land Rover, carelessly thumping them around.

Why was he so angry? Because he was overtired? Because he was told off? Because Penny was right? He told himself he didn't care and continued to remove the boxes.

Lexi and Joe turned up, clearly orchestrated to seem casual, and both started cooing over the huge amount of ammo. Ash circled them both, sniffing and casting a hopeful look at Dan. He gestured with his hand and Ash stalked back to him.

Both asked if this meant that they could do more target practice, and he agreed to ten rounds on a range every week just to stay fresh. That was overly generous, he knew, but didn't care just now. He thought to himself that he would have to stop that in a matter of weeks to conserve what they had.

They helped to carry the boxes in, and almost all of the new ammo had to be stacked in the corner of Ops, as the armoury cupboard was full.

Dan returned to the front of the Land Rover and retrieved his newest toy: the shotgun. Lexi seemed impressed and asked to have a look at it. He handed it over and had his sense of humour rewarded when she pulled a face at its stickiness.

"What the hell is all over this?" she asked.

"The former owner's brains," he said, taking it back from her and seeing her open-mouthed look of utter horror. He walked inside with Ash trotting lazily after him, casting a look to the other Rangers.

Dan shut himself away for the next few hours. He stripped, washed, scrubbed, and oiled the shotgun until no trace of blood or bone fragment remained. It classed as therapy nowadays, he supposed. He reloaded it and unloaded it, checking that the action was smooth. He liked the feel of it, and wondered if it was worth carrying as another backup weapon. He measured it against the body armour he wore, and found it to be just about short enough to draw over his shoulder if he could fashion a secure enough holster for it. He was too tired for that now, and didn't want to part with it. It was a curious-looking weapon: The folding stock went up and over the gun, and the barrel was barely an inch longer than the stock. It held five rounds, with one "in the pipe." This was definitely a tool for close encounters.

It was a silly thought – he had access to all the weapons and could set up the big machine gun in his window if he felt like it, but he wanted to keep this one close. It had something to do with it changing hands, how he had taken it from being used to take a life in sad circumstances and now was lovingly restored to protect the lives of his people. It felt symbolic to him, so he vowed to keep it. It still felt good to break some rules.

The bag of bloody equipment still needed attention, and tempted as he was to leave it, he put on a pair of rubber gloves and poured water into a plastic tub outside. He scrubbed it all with cold water and salt, turning the water pink instantly. The sidearm – a Sig Sauer identical to Dan's – had not fared well and was jammed with dried blood and tissue which had leaked down the soldier's headless body. This took some soaking to free it up before he was able to take it inside and strip it completely. He poured fresh water into the tub and added more salt, putting the kit back in to soak for longer.

He spent the afternoon in some nearby woods with a side-by-side shotgun and Ash. He got a rabbit and a pigeon for eight shots, reckoning to leave the gamekeeping to Pete.

Another hour was spent wheelbarrowing logs from the splitting pile to the store. Their winter fuel supply was coming on nicely, including bunches of twigs trimmed and bound together, but Dan thought more was needed. He reckoned winter would hit them inside of six weeks now.

Dinner was good, and more tables were occupied as the entire group was in the room. Penny called for order and welcomed Sera to the group. She finished with an announcement, not of tomorrow's tasks, but for a day of rest.

"Everyone, please meet with your departmental heads this evening at their discretion. A council meeting will be held after breakfast tomorrow, and we shall all take the day to rest and relax."

Lexi and Joe made straight for Dan as they were dismissed as such. Both were full of questions about the new routine.

"Nothing to worry about," said Dan, but he was just as curious as they were. "Find Leah and meet in Ops in ten," he said, walking out. He almost bumped into Sera in the doorway, who gave him a mocking look. He wasn't sure if she was being playful or she actually hated him.

Leah joined him at the table in Ops, followed by Lexi and Joe. Lexi poured three glasses from a bottle; Leah was obviously left out of the round. Dan sipped in satisfaction, studying the odd-shaped bottle. He rolled the liquid over his tongue and decided that he liked it. The Isle of Jura would've been somewhere he would have liked to have visited in the past. He could tell from their faces that neither Lexi nor Joe were huge Scotch fans, but neither wanted to look anything other than tough in front of him.

Ash looked up from his spot by Dan's feet to see if anyone had brought anything edible. He lay down again when he realised his luck was out.

He ran through the child-friendly version of his trip. He turned to Leah.

"Thank you for having my back with Penny. It means a lot to me," he said proudly.

Leah beamed shyly and mumbled something unintelligible.

"Where do we stand, then? I know Penny is going to want to hear our reports and plans in the morning. Joe?"

Joe looked nervous – not wanting to say something stupid was fighting a losing battle with not saying anything at all.

"Still think there should be more of us," he said. "We should have enough vehicles and kit ready for when we get recruits."

"Agreed. More Land Rovers – there are three within thirty minutes of here, as I'm lifting the ban on going south for Rangers only. You two can get those the day after tomorrow in relays. What else?"

"Army surplus store," interrupted Leah, leafing through her notebook. "There are three fairly close," she stole a small look to Lexi, who had obviously been helping her with the map work, "and I think we should take Jimmy and Kev to the biggest one…here!" she said after finding the right address on her colour-coded list.

"Good. That's good," Dan said. The machine was starting to turn, he thought as he took another sip of single malt.

"Skills gaps? Training issues?" he asked. Neither volunteered any weaknesses, which Dan recognised as a weakness in itself. "Both of you need some beefing up on breaking into places. I'm going to get some more entry kit from police stations to kit out each vehicle, but we've found that using towing chains is very effective – stick to that if possible. I've spoken with Neil, and he hopes to knock up a couple of folding anchors for us; post them through a letterbox and drive away. Simple."

Turning to Leah, Dan asked about Ops.

She blushed at being put on the spot, but said that everything was fine. "There aren't enough people to go out and not enough space to keep any more stuff we find," she explained. Fair enough assessment.

"OK, so our plan is to recover three more Defenders and lead a scavenging run to this army surplus store, which is how far away?" he asked Leah.

"Hour and a half," she shot back, "depending on traffic," she added seriously, getting a laugh from the other three.

"Good work, you three. Go do your own thing and relax tomorrow, but only after your weapons are cleaned fully and stored. Sidearms only on days off."

"Do I get a gun?" asked Leah seriously.

"No, chicken. Not yet," he said kindly.

COUNCIL OF ELDERS

Penny called for order, as formal as ever, and proceeded with the update from her perspective as Head of Home. Dan was a little miffed that she was taking overall charge of his group with less and less cooperation being sought, then thought that he didn't want the responsibility and told himself not to be childish.

"Store rooms are well stocked, and we have sufficient clothing and bedding to last the winter. Winter requirements have been ordered for logistics to retrieve, and we are well on the way to having enough wood to burn over the winter. We would welcome ideas on laundry matters, as clothes will not be disposable items forever. I feel that the staff numbers are insufficient and would seek to recruit more cleaning staff," she said. She turned to Chris and invited him to report on the agricultural matters.

"Animals are OK, got enough feed to keep them through winter, and I don't propose killing any off yet for food – need to breed them another year, I hope. I want to find a bull for the cows so we can get some milk going again. I need more people to help work the farm. Sera has already offered to check the animals, out which could take a few days," he said, uncertain in his new corporate role.

"And the gardens?" Penny asked.

"Cleared out ready to go for after Christmas when we'll get some greens and cauliflower down," he replied.

"Thank you. Neil? Engineering, if you please?" she went on.

Neil seemed tired and not the chirpy man he was when they numbered fewer. He seemed to be losing weight too.

"Vehicle workshop up and running, although touch wood," he tapped his head, "all vehicles have been fine so far. We've stockpiled parts, so I'll want them all in for a new year service. Solar panel project is on hold until we have scaffolding and builders hopefully, and an extended period of good weather to make the job safe. Rainwater collection is ongoing."

"And our fuel situation?" Penny enquired.

"Plenty," said Neil, "and nearby stocks are still high. I'll want to make another two full hauls with the tanker soon to top off the tanks on the gardens and the farm." They had discovered another large red diesel tank on the gardens.

"Thank you. Catering?" Penny looked at Cara.

"Fine," Cara said nervously. "No problems. Could do with more people in the kitchen too, I suppose."

"Medical?" Penny asked Kate.

"Staffing is good. Could still do with a surgeon, but I suppose our vet will be helpful in a pinch. Stocks are fine, but I still need to empty an A&E storeroom in a few months," Kate said.

"Supplies?" Penny looked to Andrew.

"Stores are just about full. We've started clearing other rooms to use for stockpiling also. We have food and water for our current population for maybe a year without any further scavenging," Andrew said. That was good news at least.

"James. Logistics?" Penny asked.

"All good. Point us in the direction of what you want and we're ready to go. I've been keeping mine busy by loaning them out to other areas. Doesn't hurt to know other people's jobs too," James said.

"And you are sufficiently staffed?" Penny asked.

"Until we get more space cleared for more stores, yes."

"Thank you. And lastly, Daniel. Operations," she said.

Well, bollocks to you too, he thought. If this was Penny's way of punishing him for yesterday, then she wouldn't get a rise out of him.

"Weapons and ammo levels are currently acceptable. We need more vehicles, which my Rangers will be recovering over the course of tomorrow, and after that I would like a scavenging team deployed to us for equipment recovery. I want another three Rangers ideally, and in the long term up to five security personnel based here and at the gardens. An appropriate quartermaster and a better weapons store would be ideal too," he said. "Communications are a problem; we lack the hardware and the knowledge to use any communications gear that hasn't been rendered useless by lack of maintenance on substations and satellites. High-frequency and Citizens' Band are the way forward, or backwards if you like, and we need to relearn those skills." No response from anyone. "If I may suggest, the wood we are chopping will not last this winter. It is green, and there isn't enough. Leah has located three sites for recovery of coal, which I believe are a priority over the next month. Andrew, could you source a storage area for, say, twenty to thirty tonnes?"

Andrew nodded in thought before saying, "Could Ian get another lorry? That would be sufficient to keep it from the elements, surely?" They looked to Neil, who didn't think it was a problem at all.

"Lastly," said Dan, "I want to get people out again every day. Nearly all of us have expressed a lack of personnel as a problem; we need to find more survivors, and they are unlikely to find us if we stay here all the time. The more before winter the better, because for the first time in years, the human race is going to be at risk from a simple change in weather."

All agreed, and Penny looked put out. Dan had whipped the council into a sense of urgency, of purpose, had injected some renewed need to get out and save people. He had also made suggestions that countermanded her own assessments in very slight ways.

The power struggle went on.

IT'S GOOD TO TALK

Lexi and Joe came up with a plan to maximise efficiency, which resulted in Dan dropping them off at the dealership to bring back a new Land Rover each. Time and motion.

Neil and Ian went with Adam, Jay, Kyle, Liam and Andrew. They returned late that afternoon with over five tonnes of seasoned logs from the place where they took the lorryload of bagged coal. They stacked the logs at the front of the now huge log pile to use first, and stored a lot of the coal inside in tubs ready to use. What remained went into sheds to keep dry.

Dan made another trip in the morning to take his Rangers back out for another two vehicles, and they had orders to scout for a few hours on the way back in different directions before reporting with the new Land Rovers to Neil.

He made his own recce of the army surplus store, and found so much that he had to leave it all to be a scavenging trip.

On the way back, he found himself involuntarily slowing as he stared at a thing of beauty. A vehicle parked on a driveway had caught his attention: It was very uncommon to see a new Discovery with modifications, but this one had a suspension lift, front and rear winches built into the bumpers, a snorkel, roof rack carrying jerrycans, two spare wheels, and all-terrain tyres all round. It was black, with heavily tinted back windows. He wanted it. It was actually the first thing since all this happened that he coveted. He reasoned with himself that it was functional, that it was a sensible choice, but really he just liked how it looked and wanted it.

"What do you think, boy?" he asked Ash as he scratched under his dog's chin. Ash cocked his head at him, which Dan readily took as agreement.

"All right then, but you stay here," he said as he got out.

He had barely been into a house since people started dying, but he pulled the scarf over his mouth and nose and forced the front door open. A search found the keys in a bowl on the kitchen table; he took them and left the house quickly, eager for fresh air. He climbed in and moved it to the road. He liked it: A three-litre diesel automatic was far more comfortable in his opinion than what he felt was a cramped and breezy Defender. He moved his kit into their new ride, noting how useful the heated leather seats would be when it got colder. The Defender was locked up and left on the road; he would come back to collect it on the return trip.

On the way back, he saw a vehicle moving. He was on a main road, parallel to the motorway. A lorry cab was snaking slowly along, avoiding the cars abandoned both in the lanes and on the hard shoulder. Dan checked the map quickly and reckoned he could get ahead of it within a few miles at the next junction. He followed the road signs with the blue markings and soon found himself joining the lane of what used to be a very busy road. Signs warned of delays due to ongoing improvements. Nothing new there.

His daydreaming led to a bizarre lapse in concentration, and he found himself indicating to join a motorway utterly devoid of life. He laughed at himself and rolled to a stop with his hazard lights on; he wanted the driver of that lorry to see him coming a long way off. He left Ash and the M4 in the car, and the shotgun was in the driver's door pocket. He still carried his Sig. He leaned against the side of his new vehicle and smoked as he waited for the lorry to crawl into sight.

The driver approached very cautiously, stopping some distance away and getting out with an axe held low in his right hand. Little use when facing someone with a gun, no matter how fast he was, but the statement of intent was clear.

As he approached, Dan reckoned he didn't look fast. He was at least sixty, with tanned but liver-spotted skin. A lean and leathery man with clever eyes and a wary stance.

"Blessings of God to you, friend," he said in a harsh Belfast accent.

"Good morning," Dan replied cheerily, hoping to assuage the suspicion evident in the older man's face and body language. Dan walked towards him with his hand out, and saw the man shift the axe to his left hand and move it behind him, just in case. "I promise you I mean no harm. Would you talk with me for a while?"

The older man was still very apprehensive, which he admitted to Dan. "Understand me, friend. I've met folk before now who've showed kindness and tried to take what was mine. I mean no offence by being careful."

Dan said that he understood, and told him that he had also met a few people who were dangerous. His tone implied that those people had not fared well.

"And yet you're the man standing whole in front of me," said the wise lorry driver. "Seems to me that they weren't the dangerous ones, perhaps?"

Dan smiled at his sharp logic. "Perhaps," he admitted, "but what I have done was done for the good of my people. We have a house and a farm. There are over thirty of us and we're getting ready to settle in for winter."

The man mused over this, never taking his eyes off the confident soldier who in turn kept a careful watch on the man's axe and was mindful to keep his hands away from the pistol grip on his chest.

"I'm Dan," he said, inviting a reply from the man and receiving only silence for a time.

"Jack," he said finally. "Tell me more of your home."

Dan listed off the people – those that he could remember, feeling shallow – and told Jack of the different "trades" they now had.

"Perhaps you have a spare bed for an old man?" Jack said at last.

"We do. Want to follow me?"

"I will. Do you have a CB?" Jack asked.

"A CB? No, you have one? Do you know how they work?" Dan asked excitedly.

Jack said yes to both questions. It seemed like they might get a communications network after all.

READY FOR HIBERNATION

The next week was a blur of activity. Fuel runs were made daily, until every jerrycan and fuel tank was topped to the brim. Neil even ran the generators for a couple of hours each night so that the group could sit by the heaters and watch a DVD on the large TV in the lounge area.

Dan's old Defender was recovered, and six of them were now stored in a cleared-out farm shed near the workshop. His new truck was a matter for a little jealousy, but rank had privilege, he supposed. Following the lorryload of kit taken from the army surplus store, the Rangers took over the small classroom building between the house and the gym.

Sera had checked her way through the livestock, declaring them all healthy, and logistics staff were reassigned to help with the farm animals and the cooking and cleaning to keep them busy and give others a rest. Days off were given to everyone, and the gym started to get some use.

Autumn was almost at a close then, and Dan would be lying if he said he wasn't worried about the weather. His own truck, Lexi's Land Rover, and Jimmy's lorry all had CB radios wired in and fixed to the dashboards now. Base sets were in the Ops room and at the gardens. Everyone leaving home was ordered to check every lorry they saw for a radio, and to remove it for Jack if they found one. They got a good enough signal unless masked by the terrain for at least a ten-mile radius, which Dan thought was fine for now.

The big surprise came when Joe drove back in from a trip with a heavily laden minibus behind him. Dan was in Ops when they drove in, suffering with a cold which made him groggy and irritable.

He brought in six people, all of which had found each other far to the north and decided to gather supplies before running south after the better weather. Dan was introduced to them, trying not to overtly assess their usefulness as he feigned interest.

That evening, Penny ran through her usual greeting routine. She added that she had spoken to all of the new joiners and convinced them to stay at least for the winter. She called a head-of-department meeting, and curiously one of the new women was sitting at her side when the others left.

"Karen is to be the group administrator from now on, reporting to me," she said, having to pause when Dan unintentionally interrupted with a sneeze. Karen gave a brief explanation of her work as a legal secretary and personal assistant, making her qualified to do the job. Dan smelled something funny going on, but decided to let it play out.

"As Karen knows the others better than all of us, she will run through their work assignments."

Karen smiled and started to list them.

"Jake worked in a pet store, but when offered to work with the animals, he declined. He will join the cleaning team keeping the house in order." She consulted her notes. "Carl is an electrician; I assume he will be useful to the engineering team."

She looked up at Neil, who nodded and said, "Gladly."

"Helen and Lou. Neither really have a trade, but Helen expressed a wish to work in the kitchen," she looked at Cara, who nodded, "and

Lou will be added to the cleaning team also. Steve is a helicopter pilot," she said, which got the attention of everyone at the table. She held up a hand and let everyone down gently. "He wholly believes that there will be no serviceable aircraft left by now. I'm assured that they require a lot of engineers to make one ready to fly, and it's basically an impossibility."

"Where did he learn to fly?" asked Dan.

Karen consulted her notes briefly. "He flew trips to the North Sea oil rigs," she said, and smiled at him – falsely, he suspected.

"Yes, but where did he learn?" he asked patiently.

Karen read some more before she replied, "RAF."

"I'll take him," Dan said. An RAF pilot would have some weapons training and good escape-and-evasion experience. Better than his own, most likely, having never faced the prospect of being shot down and alone behind enemy lines.

"He has expressed a wish to –" Karen started in disagreement.

"Let me speak to him, then. If he doesn't want to be a Ranger, then that's fine," Dan said with finality.

Penny took over again, smiling at him to show to everyone that there was no animosity. "Very well, everyone. Is there any other business?" she asked.

"Weather is closing in. Very soon we will be limited to off-road vehicles on short trips and tractors or walking between here and the farm," Dan said, looking around the table for agreement and getting it from everyone. "When the frosts and snow start, the only people to leave home regularly will be Rangers, and they will work in pairs. I know we've all driven in ice and snow before, but without any road maintenance, a simple journey will be far more dangerous. One Ranger will always be here for protection, though." Nobody disagreed, and the council melted away.

He decided to offer an olive branch to Penny, as she still hadn't forgiven him. "We get through this winter, we'll do fine," he said.

Penny smiled warmly at him, and said, "We will, I'm sure of it."

Dan left the meeting, bumping into Leah and sending her to find Steve and bring him to Ops. She was annoyed, as they were about to turn the power on for the TV, but he promised her a surprise in the morning. Easily distracted, she skipped off, and Dan sat in Ops to pour two glasses.

Steve was maybe forty-five, fit and still with a totally full head of hair. Dan was annoyed at that because the man had nearly ten years on him, and he had had to shave his hair and beard to the same length, exposing his rapidly receding hairline. Steve knew he was getting the sales pitch but kept his face neutrally interested.

Dan asked about his early career, finding out that Steve had flown numerous different types of helicopters over the last quarter century, having spent almost the last nine months in his retirement playing taxi in godawful weather in a Sea King.

His early training and operational deployments had indeed covered highly in-depth escape-and-evasion training. Some of it was delivered not far from where they were at an army camp in the nineties.

Dan knew it fairly well.

He spoke a little of what the Rangers were expected to do, and some of the highlights of recent events.

"I'm not going to piss about; I want you on board," he said after a thoughtfully long sip of Scotch.

"I was always going to say yes," Steve said, and stood to drain the last of his glass. "Thanks for the drink. I assume I start in the morning?"

"Yes. See you after breakfast."

THE DEMONS WE CARRY

The patient didn't remember much. He knew of dark things in his past. Of pain and incarceration. Of white halls and white floors and white coats. Of injections and tablets.

He did remember that he never felt so alive as when they stopped making him take the tablets. When they coughed, spluttered, and lay down to die. He did not die. The demon who controlled him had kept him alive for a reason.

He walked along the hospital corridors for days, staring, touching and resting when he felt the need. He took clothes from people and other possessions as he wandered between wards and cubicles without challenge. He enjoyed the quiet and the freedom.

He received instruction from the demon. It told him of great plans he had now that all those who would stand in his way were dead – killed by its own power, it claimed. The man did what the demon told him.

At some time in the second week of him walking the corridors, the demon told him to feed from the body of a once beautiful young doctor. Her beauty would be added to theirs if he ate it.

The cycle went on for weeks like this. Twice he did as he was commanded and ate the flesh of those the demon wanted to absorb into their body. He heard the demon tell him to look in the mirror, that he could see the change already in them.

As he walked the now familiar halls one day, he heard the sound of smashing glass. The demon bid him to go and see what caused the intrusion into their domain.

He stalked slowly towards them, powerful and lithe like a predator.

He saw his prey, and the demon told him how to take her.

TAKE YOUR SHILLING, MAKE YOUR MARK

Steve's firearms assessment was a formality, as was sorting and issuing his personal kit. Dan just watched as he put the gear together effectively. Lexi and Joe put their heads around the door to say goodbye and welcome their new "brother" before they went on the last scouting missions of the week, and probably this year. Lexi was to check out A&E to see if it was viable to scavenge there yet, and Joe was checking lorry parks for more CB radios plus whatever else he found.

Steve was skilled behind the wheel and was given Dan's old Defender. He took a similar gun to Dan too: a carbine with a suppressor and a mid-range zoom optic. He carried himself and his equipment like a professional, which pleased Dan to no end. Somehow having another trained man holding a gun made him feel better, less like the responsibility was a burden.

Dan spent some time fashioning the end of a gun slip into a holster for the shotgun to sit diagonally along his back. Steve had recognised it as a SPAS, nodding with approval. Dan only found out what it was by reading the etchings by the trigger guard, but he knew how it worked and thought he had seen it used in a film or two. Lou, one of the new women, found him wandering the house looking for sewing supplies. He explained what he wanted to do and she traded conversation for needlework. Dan was happy to oblige, and after some time spent chatting over coffee, she had produced a black tube to fit the gun with heavy elastic sewn in to keep it secure. She used some attachments from an unused kit to fashion the fixings, making it removable if needed, and it fit the back of his vest perfectly.

He was feeling satisfied with life and looking forward to rabbit-and-pigeon pie tonight with some beers and cake before settling down for a film by the heaters.

All these plans were shattered and his good mood disintegrated when Lexi failed to come back that evening.

He told the concerned gathering that he was sure Lexi was fine, that it was probably a vehicle fault or something. He told them all to go to bed and that he would go first thing in the morning to where she was sent. Leah said she went to check the nearest hospital, about ten miles away as the crow flies.

Dan was worried. Very worried. She should easily be within CB range, and no transmission was made or replied to. She could be in a black spot. Could she have had vehicle failure? No, she could've walked back here hours ago. The more he thought of it, the more worried he became. He was sure she had met something hostile.

He waited until his audience had left Ops, then broke out his carbine, shotgun and sidearm. He had three full magazines for the 9mm Sig Sauer, five full magazines of 5.56 for his suppressed M4, and six shells locked and loaded into the shotgun strapped to his back. Close encounters.

Ash watched him in silence. He knew something was up and was waiting for the word to move. That dog got bigger every day and would be fully grown by Christmas. His paws were still too big for him, though.

Dan went to sneak out, and was blocked by Steve in the doorway. He too was dressed fully in black with a black tactical vest filled with magazines. He carried the same weapons as Dan, with his equipment almost identical, although his was black and Dan's was tan-coloured. Dan's individual eccentricity was the rare stubby shotgun; that was his legacy from a story he didn't want to share yet.

"I assumed we were moving straight away?" Steve asked.

"Yes. Take these; I'm guessing I don't need to show you how they work?" Dan replied, sliding a black Peli case across the table towards him. A pair of night-vision goggles was inside, which Steve was familiar with. God only knew how he flew a helicopter wearing them, Dan thought.

"We'll go in mine," Dan said, and walked out of the front door to the ornate building they called home. "Heel," he growled softly as he went, and the grey dog shot out after him to walk at his left side before jumping into the black Land Rover Discovery, heading out into the gathering dark.

Dan had put a stop to moving at night for the prime reason that the sight and sound of a vehicle moving in the dark nowadays was about as noticeable as a fireworks display.

He drove slowly, using the night-vision goggles to see, as he had no lights on. These were fine with practice, but the lack of depth perception made everything after about thirty metres a surprise. That kept you on your toes.

He was cursing himself for not giving in to his paranoia and pulling out all the bulbs on his new off-roader. He had to make do with strips of heavy gaffer tape over all the light clusters, but was still sure that some of the brightness escaped. Maybe one of his brainiacs could develop a kill switch to knock off all the fuses to the bulbs.

He forced himself to concentrate on the perilous drive and not worry about the things outside of his control. There was nothing to say for certain that Lexi was in trouble, but he felt that this was serious; she went dark way too close to home for comfort.

Steve sat in the passenger's seat checking a map by the light of a small red-lensed torch. Dan didn't need many directions, as the road signs still stood, but Steve was being thorough and studying the map for knowledge and possibilities.

Dan killed the engine about a mile short of the hospital and looked at the map, with Steve whispering points of reference and interest to him. Both had their goggles pushed up on their heads to allow some night vision to develop, as it was now nearing pitch-black.

Steve pointed to a place on the map and said "ERV," meaning emergency rendezvous point. "Wait one hour and return to the vehicle. Leave the keys on the rear nearside wheel," he finished.

"Agreed," said Dan, meaning that if they got split up and the other did not make it to the meeting point, then they would be left behind by the other. Losing one could easily turn into losing three. Losing these three in particular would almost certainly mean death or hardship for the group.

They stalked in slowly, working as a pair: One covered as the other moved. They performed this leapfrogging, Ash gliding silently by Dan's side, until they reached the approach to the hospital.

They spent some time watching the building as best as they could and saw no movement. They began to leapfrog forward again, more slowly now.

Dan took cover and scanned the ground ahead. He thought he could smell the hospital from here already. He froze, double-checked what he thought he saw, and then snapped his fingers once for Steve's attention. He remained in position, weapon pointing towards the interest until Steve moved to his side and whispered in his ear.

"Hers?" he asked.

"Yes," Dan whispered back. Ash let out the smallest of whines, and Dan quieted him with a reassuring hand on the back of his head. Dan had seen the Land Rover that he had given to Lexi – a grey Defender with black wheels and a black roof, chunky off-road tyres, and a solid metal-sided boot space. A chill washed over him, a wave of fear and responsibility.

"Go slow, and do a three sixty until we find an access point," he whispered, intending to retrace Lexi's steps.

"Roger," Steve responded, and went first.

They started from nearest her vehicle, as would make sense, to see if and where she had got inside. The Defender was parked by the main front doors, and they worked to the left where they found the A&E entrance after a couple of hundred metres.

Smashed glass in a defunct sliding door said she was likely in. It didn't look like old damage at all, and only a few leaves had blown inside. Dan was concerned about taking Ash in through the broken glass, so spent ten painstaking and leg-cramping minutes brushing it away slowly to avoid making noise. All the time, Steve was scanning all around him, alert for signs of danger.

Ash was a great early warning system; his ears and nose would detect people and noises long before they could, and Dan had learned to take his lead from the adolescent dog at times like this. Not that his nose would be much use inside – the air hung heavy, rank with the choking smell of decomposing bodies.

When he had finally cleared their entrance, he whispered, "Moving" softly to Steve.

He climbed inside as silently as possible before leading Ash through. He made him sit in the waiting room, confident that nothing would get to them and still possess all its limbs intact.

They went as silently as possible, having to use the goggles, as the inside of the building allowed no ambient light to penetrate. Dan wished he had some green dot laser sights for the carbine, but had never considered he might have to do building searches by goggles. He snapped himself out of the brief daydream. Ash was blinded by the darkness, but his canine senses were worth an entire squad of trained special forces right now.

It took a long time to clear even a small area in a tight formation of three, but neither suggested splitting up – it was too dangerous to contemplate.

A low growl came from Ash, quickly stopped as Dan put a reassuring hand down to him. He could hear the dog sniffing the ground, and looked down to decipher the marks he could see.

There were streaks of dried blood – but then there were rotting bodies and blood trails in a lot of places – but this was fresh, red, not brown. Dan looked closer and saw two parallel dark lines mixed in with the blood trail. He ran his finger over them, and was rewarded with the tiny shreds of rubber balling up under his touch.

He turned to whisper to Steve, "Bleeding. Dragged. Boots left rubber marks." Steve bent to examine the same and offered no other explanation. He nodded, and Dan followed the tracks slowly with Ash stalking silently beside him. Deeper they went into the pitch-black heart of the foul hospital.

LET US PREY

The patient had seen the woman walking carefully through the hospital. He followed her on bare feet, moving like a ghost. He was a hunter, and she was his prey. She carried a gun on her back and had one in her hands which she pointed everywhere she looked.

The demon told him that she was dangerous, but that he could not let her violate their temple of death. *Take her*, the voice urged. *Take her now!*

The patient picked up a heavy box by the handle, silently, carefully. He walked behind her as she opened cupboards and looked for things. She could not be allowed to desecrate this place any longer. He stepped out silently and readied himself like a cat.

The woman froze and started to turn towards him, raising her gun.

He swung the heavy box, hitting her on the left temple at the same moment she saw him and her eyes went wide with fear.

Yes, said the demon. *Fear us*, he shouted as she slumped to the floor and dropped her gun. The man stood there, breathing deeply with exultation at his prowess as a predator. He looked down on the woman and marvelled at her youth and beauty. She was dressed as a warrior, but he had bested her easily.

He took her gun, caressing it as a tool of power over others, before he took her by the wrists and dragged her limp body through his lair.

He tied her to the walls using the wires and tubes, making intricate patterns as he built a shrine to her body. The demon told him what to do at every turn, purring his orders to the man and enjoying every second.

She will be perfect for us, it said.

He used the woman's knife to cut away her clothing, inspecting each piece as he removed it until she hung slumped in her bindings, naked and dripping blood from her head onto the floor.

He watched her until the light grew pale. When it started to get dark, he lit candles taken from the chapel where he had torn the heavy wooden cross from the wall. *He holds no power here*, warned the demon, *only I.*

He inspected her thoroughly, feeling a desire he had not felt for as long as he could remember. *Not yet*, instructed the demon. *She is mine to take and you will not touch her until I command.*

The patient made slow, almost lazy cuts along the top of her breasts, watching with fascination as the blood ran to form a small puddle next to the one made of the blood from her head. He watched in blissful anticipation as the drops formed on her nipple, holding his breath until it fell to the ground. He was so silent and intent that he could hear the drips falling.

He was readying himself to take her, to consume her and make her part of him, when he heard an animal noise in the dark catacombs of the hospital.

He took no chances and moved to hide where he could still see his prize. He would kill whatever came for him, and then take her.

They crept through the corridor, following the faint trail of what they feared and suspected was the path of one of their own.

The dog made the first move, becoming the catalyst for a violent sequence of events.

Ash's hackles rose, and he let out an echoing growl of bloodcurdling menace that gave the men goosebumps. Dan hissed at him to heel with no response. He moved forward a pace and put his hand on the dog's back. He was rewarded by Ash's response to turn and snap at him.

He recoiled. He had never seen Ash so tense, so scared and so dangerous. He took a pace in front of the animal and repeated "No" as loud as he dared. The dog did not back down, but at least he went silent. Dan could no longer trust Ash not to give away their position. He had to make a decision that he wasn't happy with: To leave him there and go on without his capabilities.

He told him to stay in a hissed growl, and the dog reluctantly lowered himself to the ground without taking his eyes off him.

Dan turned to Steve, who watched intently. Fear showed on the former pilot's face, and he was certain he mirrored the same emotions. Dan could barely control his breathing and wanted to give in to the panic. To run from the hospital. If he did, he was certain that they would not see Lexi alive again.

They proceeded another twenty, thirty, forty metres along the mile-long corridor that seemed to be the spine of the building, like it was a living organism. Steve held up a hand and sniffed the air. He whispered close to Dan's ear, "Smoke. Candles."

Dan removed his goggles and saw the faintest glow of light from a doorway ahead and to their right. Something or someone was there, and they would have walked right past it with their goggles on. He showed Steve what he intended with hand signals, and the two began to stalk towards the doorway as silently as possible.

They reached the doorway and pushed the goggles up to their heads. Both had been moving for over two hours now, all of that time under huge mental and physical pressure. The corridor past them was lit with a flickering yellow light. Using hand signals, he told Steve what he wanted to do. Steve nodded and went in first, low and slow with the carbine up at the ready. It took an eternity to reach the end of the corridor, and when they did, neither could contain their pent-up fear and rage any longer.

Steve cried out "NO" and burst into the room where Lexi was tied naked to the wall in a sickening effigy of crucifixion. The left side of her face was a mask of dark and swollen skin, and blood ran freely from carvings on her chest. As Dan went to call a warning and pull him back, the patient struck.

He slashed Steve deeply across the left forearm with Lexi's knife, making him drop his weapon. The patient followed up with a vicious upswing of the pistol in his left hand, catching him under the chin and sprawling him backwards onto the cold floor.

He seemed surprised to see Dan, but threw himself at him like a wild animal. The patient was filthy, and the stink of him was rank in

Dan's nostrils as he stepped back to avoid the attack. He was naked and matted with blood, but holding a razor-sharp knife in one hand and a gun in the other.

He was on Dan too fast for him to use the carbine, and he was forced to push it out in front of him to ward off the vile creature. The knife came low and lethal at him underneath his pathetic barrier, and caught him fully in the abdomen. The body armour was sufficient to stop the blade from disembowelling him, but the force of the impact drove the air from his lungs and hurt him.

He had no time to recover from this before the knife came down from up high and slashed him from head to chin. He was blinded instantly by his own hot blood in his eyes, and he screamed in rage and terror as he hauled the disgusting beast off him and threw him to the side. Dan couldn't see, and the sound of his pulse banging in his ears deafened him to the small sounds that could help him locate their attacker. He hit the floor hard, banging the back of his head and bringing bile to his throat immediately. He knew he was badly damaged.

On instinct, he used his sleeve desperately to try to wipe the blood away, but it was replaced instantly with more and his brain registered only a snapshot of his attacker preparing to fly at him again.

He was sure he had failed: He had failed to train Lexi well enough to ensure her survival, he had failed to protect his newest recruit who had trusted him enough to come, he had failed to trust his most loyal friend, and he had failed to kill the beast who threatened the lives of them all.

He felt sad and helpless, wondering at the point of all their suffering if the brutal nature of their futile struggle was to end them here in this stinking mausoleum.

The resounding thud of bodily impact snapped him from his self-pitying reverie of submission.

The noises that accompanied the thud told him that help had arrived and given them all a chance of survival. The sound of snarling and ripping flesh betrayed the ferocity and desperation of Ash's attack. He heard the sound of wild man and dog rolling only feet away from him, and fought to clear the blood from his eyes. He tore desperately at the matting mess on his face with his hands as the man fell on him again. Dirty fingers clawed at him; foul breath was in his face. He fought to roll on his side, reaching for the shotgun over his shoulder with his right hand. He was blinded and had never felt more desperate.

A horribly loud and pained yelp told him that Ash was hurt, the cry of his dog cutting through to his very soul.

He had to act now to use the time gifted to him by his loyal companion, or they were all dead. He rolled, pulling the ugly shotgun from its elasticated holster over his shoulder as he got to one knee. Flicking the safety catch by feel, he yelled, "DOWN, ASH!" waited a second, as long as he dared, and fired.

Three deafening booms echoed around the dead hospital, interspersed with the metallic sounds on the pump-action replacing the chambered shells. He fired in an arc, left to right, in an upward direction, praying to hit only the wild man. He could hear nothing but the high-pitched ringing of his shocked eardrums, then silence.

EPILOGUE

Dan lay there panting, light-headed. He was barely conscious and terrified.

He struggled back to his feet and tried to wipe the blood from his eyes again. He groped around and found a rag of a hospital gown that he wrapped around his head and left eye. He sucked water from the bladder built into his vest and spat it into his hand to give him at least some vision out of his right eye.

There was no sign of the man they'd fought with and so nearly lost to. Blood was all over the floor and he could not tell whose it was. He staggered forwards to find Steve unconscious and bleeding heavily from a deep cut to his left forearm. He found another gown and tied it tight around the wound before going to Lexi.

She was still alive, but her pulse was weak. He cut her down and wrapped her in a white blanket. He tried to lift her, but fell twice, weak from blood loss and pain. He eventually rolled both Lexi and Steve into another blanket he had laid on the floor, and dragged them together as he crawled to retrace their steps. He had to get help before he passed out, as his injuries threatened the end for all of them.

He called for his dog desperately, fearing the worst, but he did not come, and Dan could not find him.

He made maybe thirty metres along the endless corridor before he lost consciousness, only to regain it with a gasp after he knew not how long.

Seemingly for hours he laboured, dragging the inanimate forms of his two friends and crying with the pain at the fate of his absent dog.

He eventually made it back to where they had all entered at different times, and could go no further. Light was beginning to show at the edge of the sky now, and he tried one last effort with what remained of his strength.

He dragged himself through the smashed glass panel, being cut again, as he lacked the alertness to avoid the glass shards. He pulled himself towards Lexi's vehicle as his peripheral vision began to fade.

He hauled himself to the side step, then the door handle, and tried the door. Barely able to believe his luck, he found the door open and tried to get inside, where he grabbed the speaker mic of the CB radio.

He keyed the press-to-talk, calling weakly for anyone who would be listening. "Help us," he gasped. "Hospital," and slumped into the foot well, finally unconscious for good.

Very few of the group had believed Dan's assertion that all was well, and it was no secret that he left not long after with Steve, both heavily armed. Loud disputes had gone on through the night, with Neil and Joe advocates of going after them with everything they had.

Penny raised strong counterarguments, supported by the lefties and the pacifists and those in favour of a warm bed and a clear conscience through their blinkered views.

Jack had remained mute throughout, carefully watching the CB radio for any twitch of life. For hours he sat as the arguments raged around him.

Kate had prepared her ambulance for a rescue mission, and was arguing for action over inaction. Penny finally went too far by declaring, "He only has himself to blame if he has gone out and found trouble. He has a habit of doing so!"

That was too much for Neil. "Do you think any of us would be here if not for him?" he turned and yelled at her, taut with anger.

Mike, more through personal experience and loyalty than his own beliefs, sided with Neil. "He has killed to keep us safe, and you would just abandon him?" he asked angrily, very conscious that he would be dead and his daughter brutalised if Dan and Lexi had not saved them.

A shout from Jack silenced them all. "QUIET," he roared, and turned back to the radio set.

"Say again," he spoke into the mic. "Repeat. Dan, are you there, friend?"

Nothing.

He turned to the group, still frozen in their stances of mid-argument. "I heard them. He said 'Help. Hospital.' I'd have heard more but for your howling," he said, looking at Penny with obvious scorn. "I, for one, am going. Now. Who is with me?" he said as he nodded to Joe.

Joe led the way in his Land Rover with Jack. Kate followed in the ambulance with Neil riding, quite literally, shotgun.

They were at the hospital by daybreak, arriving in the biggest contrast to Dan and Steve, and what they saw made them fear the worst.

Joe was out of the car and scanning wildly with his rifle, moving towards Dan. Kate nearly bowled Joe over to get to Dan first, checking his pupil response and shouting his name. He came round enough to speak.

"Inside. Help the others," he said before blacking out again.

He slipped away into the dark, and knew nothing more.

The story continues in AFTER IT HAPPENED BOOK 2: HUMANITY

A message from the author

Thanks for reading. Please leave a review on Amazon if you enjoyed it!

You can find me on:

Twitter: @DevonFordAuthor

Facebook: Devon C Ford Author

Subscribe to my email list and read my blog:

www.devonfordauthor.uk

Printed in Great Britain
by Amazon